"Darcy, I hate to tell you this."

Given the expression on Garret's face, Darcy really did not want to hear the news he had to deliver. "All the motels and hotels are booked."

"Still?" What was she going to do? She had no car and nowhere to stay.

"The power companies have come to town to take care of the outages. Every open room has been promised to them. You're going to have to stay here another night."

"I can't stay at your house." Heat flooded her cheeks. "The woman who called you earlier... Jocelyn? Garret, I don't want to mess anything up with you and her. Surely she was upset about my being here. Did you explain?"

"Yes, I explained and everything is fine."

She seriously doubted that. No woman with an attachment to Garret would be fine with another woman in his house, sleeping in his *bed*. Pregnant or not.

Dear Reader,

With my pregnancies I experienced the terror of premature labor pains and all the thoughts and fears that run rampant in a new mother's head. I had the loving support of my husband (and, yes, our children were both fine), but Darcy Rhodes isn't so lucky. She's pregnant, alone, stuck in a strange town with an uncertain future.

But the one *good* that happens to her is meeting Garret Tulane. Garret is an all-around nice guy. Of course nice guys have problems, too, and since he's already dating his boss's daughter, well, complicated doesn't begin to describe things. Is it possible to care for and love two women? I didn't think so, but then I saw a real-life example of this and realized with the right hero, it's entirely possible. Eventually a choice has to be made, but by the time Garret makes it, will Darcy be gone?

I hope you enjoy *Another Man's Baby*. It's the first of a series titled THE TULANES OF TENNESSEE, and I'm looking forward to writing about many more Tulanes in the future. Nick is coming up next with all his sexy brooding and secrets. Who isn't curious about a guy with secrets?

Your letters and comments mean the world to me, so please keep writing. I love to hear from you. E-mail me at kay@kaystockham.com, write to me at P.O. Box 232, Minford, OH 45653 and check out my Web site by surfing to www.kaystockham.com. I hope you'll join me.

God bless and enjoy the romance,

Kay Stockham

ANOTHER MAN'S BABY
Kay Stockham

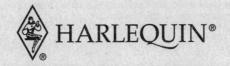

HARLEQUIN®

TORONTO • NEW YORK • LONDON
AMSTERDAM • PARIS • SYDNEY • HAMBURG
STOCKHOLM • ATHENS • TOKYO • MILAN • MADRID
PRAGUE • WARSAW • BUDAPEST • AUCKLAND

ISBN-13: 978-0-373-78222-2
ISBN-10:   0-373-78222-5

ANOTHER MAN'S BABY

ABOUT THE AUTHOR

Best parenting advice ever received? Oh, hands down the best advice was to let my kids entertain themselves. I did it from day one. Even when they were little, my children were content exploring the area around them while I worked. It gave me a lot of writing time. **Mrs. Brady or Mrs. Cleaver?** Mrs. Brady. Any woman who can talk her husband into having a housekeeper when she isn't employed deserves all the pampering she can get! **Cloth or disposable?** Disposable! **Favorite quote from your mom?** "Because I said so!" I use that one a lot. <G> **If you could've kept your child at a specific age, what would that be?** I'd have to say between nine and twelve months. They were just learning how to talk, crawl and walk but were still snuggly with Mom. Such a fun, fun age. **Most poignant moment with your own bundle of joy?** Holding them for the first time. After waiting so long for them to arrive, going through the tests and the trials of pregnancy, holding them was sweet indeed. **What makes a mom?** Being able to love your child no matter the mood they're in. A mom can control only so much—the rest is in God's hands. But the mood swings of adolescents? That takes true love.

To Jessica Bird/J. R.Ward for describing
the many aspects of Garret's job. You *rock!*

CHAPTER ONE

PAIN SURROUNDED her pregnant stomach and sharpened with knifelike intensity. Darcy Rhodes swallowed once, twice, as the threat of hurling abated along with the cramp that had taken her so by surprise.

Sliding into the narrow, Tennessee mountain road's salt-rusted guardrail hadn't been fun, but at least she'd stopped with a fairly light, if jarring, jolt. For a split second midskid, she'd wondered if she would plunge right over the edge.

You just had to keep driving to make up for the pee stops, didn't you?

She collapsed against her Volkswagen's seat, barely daring to breathe for fear that the pain would return or, worse, the movement would cause the guardrail to break and send her hurtling down the mountainside. Before the cramp had hit she'd done little more than reassure herself that she hadn't been severely injured—all body parts were still attached—and all four wheels appeared to be on solid, if slippery, ground. But now…

Now what?

The passenger-side air bag had deployed on impact and sagged across the dash like a deflated balloon. Chalky powder filled the air, making her nose itch and her throat burn. Who *wouldn't* tense up and react to what had happened?

She took a deep, cleansing breath, coughing weakly because of the powder. The cramp was just that, a mixture of fright and the need to pee. A normal reaction. As soon as she twisted the keys in the ignition the car would start and she would be on her way once again, slowly but surely. The very first hotel she saw, no matter how dirty, smelly or disgusting, she would stop without a single complaint.

The steady stream of freezing rain quickly changed over to a sleet-snow mix, and she watched, dazed, while the little bits of ice globbed together on her windshield before slowly sliding toward the hood.

Ignoring the weather as best she could, Darcy grasped the keys and turned. Nothing. Not even a stutter. She tried again. And again. *Nothing?*

She stared out the moisture-blurred windshield, her mind too full to think clearly. Mostly because it flashed to the horror flicks she'd watched as a kid. She knew what happened to stranded motorists— they were always the first victims. Back then she'd clamped her hands over her eyes to escape the scary parts, but there was no escaping this. When had she last seen a car? Twenty minutes? Half an hour? "They had better sense and stopped somewhere."

And now you're talking to yourself. Someone will be along soon.

But when? Darcy groaned, all too aware the passenger door was a lot closer than it had been five minutes ago, and shifted to find her cell phone. When she couldn't, she leaned over to peer into the dim abyss of the passenger floor, the shadow she cast negating the illumination offered by the overhead light. At least her air bag hadn't deployed and she hadn't hit the console between the seats. If she had, she could've broken a rib, and her baby—

Not going to go there, she told herself firmly. "Everything is fine." Her thick coat and the pillow she used for comfort had cushioned the impact.

Finally spotting the phone lying near an empty sour-cream-and-onion chips bag, she managed to snag it, only to swear at the illuminated display. She shook the phone, held it up in various spots in the interior of the car, but the little bars indicating signal strength didn't budge.

Her mind chose that moment to flash on an image of the movie heroine having car trouble and a strange man appearing out of nowhere and offering to help, the bowie knife concealed until it's too late.

Stop it!

Darcy turned off the overhead light and stared out

at the landscape revealed by her one remaining headlight. At least the battery still worked. It didn't power the heat, but she wouldn't have to sit in total darkness while her mind ran amok.

Cold seeped into the car with every gusty blow of wind, the battered little Bug rocking with the force. *And when the bough breaks?*

"Nothing's going to break. You're not going to—"

Something struck the rear, the *thump* startling her so badly her breath hitched in her throat. What was *that?*

She jerked around to look out the back window, the side mirrors, but saw nothing. The wind in the trees? A twig or branch? The road was littered with them, the combination of the wind and precipitation wreaking havoc on the area. Just her luck, she would have to get lost in the stupid forest.

Darcy double-checked the locks on the doors. If she jumped and tensed at every little sound, she'd be a basket case in no time. Maybe music would help? She turned the knob.

"And now a weather update…" Two seconds after finding a station, she groaned. In typical weather-man style, they'd gotten it wrong. The forecasted dusting of snow was now a full-fledged winter-storm advisory, and she was right in the middle of it with a car that wouldn't start and no cell service.

Where *was* everyone? Surely there was someone

out on the roads. "Where's a cop when you actually need one?" She shoved her hair behind her ear, but it sprang right back.

"Be prepared for the worst," the too-chipper radio voice added. "We're in for a doozy. Stay indoors and conserve heat. Power outages are being reported throughout the listening area, and repair crews are running behind. For further updates and information, stay tuned. Up next is everyone's favorite, 'Don't worry, be happy.'"

Darcy rolled her eyes and turned the radio off with an angry twist of the knob. This couldn't be happening. Seriously, how many people got stuck like this?

Bands of muscle began to contract, up her back and around her middle. No, no, no. This was not happening. It was too soon.

She fought the pain, tensing, then just as quickly tried to will the muscles lax. She was fine. *They* were fine. It was only a cramp. The phone in one hand, she rubbed her belly, noted that it was hard as a rock and getting harder, the ache in her back growing sharper and more uncomfortable. "It's just a cramp," she whispered, eyes squeezed tight. Slow, deep breaths. In and out. Calm. Soothing. She gave massages for a living, she knew soothing. She could *do* soothing. It was mind over matter.

"Just calm down. A car w-will be along soon, and

this—" she exhaled, blowing the air out of her mouth "—is just a cramp…. Just an itsy-bitsy cra— *Ohhh!*"

The phone clattered as it hit the floor. Her hands fumbled, finally latching on to the steering wheel. She squeezed hard, a low moan escaping her lips she couldn't have held back if her life depended on it.

Finally the contraction—oh, God help her, they really *were* contractions!—subsided and that's when pure, unadulterated fear kicked in. No cell signal. Lost because of a wrong turn, stranded in the mountains in a snowstorm and—*in labor?*

"Oh, God, please. It's been a while. Okay, I know, it's been a long, *long* time, but please—" She bit her lip, unable to deny the truth any longer. "Help me. I can't do this here. I can't do this *alone.* I need help. *Please,* I need help!"

Time passed, minutes blurring together as contractions came and went. She remained where she was, her grip tight on the wheel, eyes closed during the worst of the pain when it felt as though her body was being shredded from back to front. Oh, please. Please, please, ple—

Bang-bang-bang!

The pounding on Darcy's car roof scared her so badly she shrieked and leaned sideways in the bucket seat to escape. How had she missed seeing the headlights of the vehicle stopped beside her car?

I've told you a million times, child. Ask and ye

shall receive. Believe and, if it's His will, you'll be just fine.

She blinked, dazed by the combination of pain, surprise and the memory of her grandmother's voice.

"Hey," a man's voice called, "you okay in there?" *Bang, bang.* "Need some help?"

"Please don't let him have a knife." Her pain-tensed body tightened even more when she spied the large shadow looming outside her window. But what choice did she have?

Hoping Nana was right, Darcy flipped the lock, fumbled with the handle and pushed weakly, but the door didn't budge. She hit it with her palm.

Apparently catching on that the door wasn't opening, the man yanked twice before it gave with a shattering explosion of ice. "Are you all right?"

Unable to respond because the contraction hit its peak, she bit her lip and shook her head because it was all she could manage.

"Are you hurt?" The man's tone was more insistent.

She reached out and grabbed his overcoat to make sure he didn't leave and the soft, expensive feel of the cloth registered at the same time the banded muscles finally loosened their grip on her body. She fell against her seat in relief.

The man bent into the car, effectively blocking the opening and shielding her from the worst of the weather. She caught a brief sniff of his cologne.

The dome light above their heads didn't illuminate much, but she was able to make out dark, close-trimmed hair, thick brows, a longish nose and the shaded roughness of lightly stubbled cheeks. He had to be gorgeous, didn't he?

His lips were turned down at the corners in a concentrated scowl, his expression clearly worried and concerned rather than threatening. A little of her anxiety eased, but not all. *If you sent me an angel, Nana, this one has black wings.*

"Where do you hurt?"

"I…I'm p-p— Oh, no." She moaned when another contraction made itself known, and vaguely heard her handsome rescuer mutter something indistinguishable when he realized the lump between her and the steering wheel wasn't just the bulk of her coat.

"You're *pregnant?*"

She managed a nod, imagining she heard his deep voice squeak a bit there at the end.

"Okay, uh— How far apart are the contractions?"

This pain ended fairly quickly and wasn't as intense as before. That was a good thing. Right? She released the air from her lungs in a gush. "They're…c-close together b-but irregular."

A glove-warmed hand brushed the hair off her forehead. He had calluses on his fingers, not thick or abrasive but there; something she wouldn't have guessed him to have, given his expensive appearance.

"How far along are you? Any special conditions? Who's your doctor?"

She struggled to focus on the questions. "I...I don't have a doctor. Not here. I'm on my way to Indiana." Her grip tightened on his coat. "I *can't* have the baby *here!*" She felt herself weakening, the fear she'd barely managed to keep locked away breaking free.

"Hey, no tears. Come on, sweetheart, don't do that to me," the man murmured. He brushed his thumb over her cheek.

The gesture had a calming effect, and even though her body ached and everything had gone wrong, she felt a connection with him.

Because he's the only thing standing between you and self-delivery. Did you even look *for a knife?*

"Stay still, okay? I'll go call for help. Don't move."

Like she could go anywhere else. The guy straightened and the door closed sharply, carried by the wind. The slam caused more ice to crack, and a small sheet slid down the windshield where it wedged beneath the wiper blade, obliterating her ability to see.

This was what it was like to suffocate. To feel hemmed in and confined, surrounded by darkness.

Melodramatic much? Just stay calm. All she had to do was keep it together and ignore the pain spreading along her back. Relax. *Breathe.* But what if the man didn't return? What if he went back to his car and drove away because he didn't want the responsibility of helping her? How many people *would* help her? Had it been someone else by the side of the road and her driving by, would she have stopped?

She gripped the steering wheel so tightly her fingers went numb. Then, as fast as it had come on her, the contraction ended, the tension subsiding to a dull ache.

Darcy huddled in her seat, cold in a hot and shivery, this-really-can't-be-happening kind of way. The baby would be fine. She had to believe that. She couldn't believe anything else because if she did—

She caught a glimpse of movement in her peripheral vision, unable to believe what she was seeing. The man's vehicle was *moving*.

Darcy straightened in the seat, her heart racing out of control the way it had when she'd been the new kid on the merry-go-round the bullies had tried to sling off. She flattened her hands on the window. Pounded on the glass. Her sweaty palms left prints behind. "Wait! Wait, don't leave!"

But the large vehicle drove on.

Images came again. First Stephen, his parents, the storm and the accident. The baby and now this. She dropped her forehead to the cold glass, fighting the cramping sensation as long as she could.

I asked, Nana. I asked! What now?

The contraction leaped from cramp status to uncomfortable, this-really-hurts *pain*. What now?

All she wanted was to give her baby the best life possible, make up for screwing up the beginning of its life. A nice home, someplace safe. Maybe a nice guy somewhere down the line. To *be* the mother—

You don't know how to be?

She wrapped her arms around her stomach and rocked. "*Please*...don't leave me."

CHAPTER TWO

GARRET TULANE DROVE past the little Volkswagen to a straightaway, then carefully began the arduous task of turning his large SUV around on the slippery, narrow road.

The conditions were dangerous no matter how good a driver was and, glimpsing the Florida tags on the newer model VW, he doubted the woman inside had a lot of experience with snow and mountains.

The attorney in him balked at the potential lawsuit she could file if something happened to her or the baby while in his care, but what else could he do? People bit the hand extended to help them all the time. It was a risk he had to take.

With the Escalade in position Garret got out, the blast of cold air actually feeling good on his adrenaline-heated body. Leave it to him to stumble upon a pregnant woman on a night like this.

He pulled open the VW's door and, for the second time that night, he inhaled evergreens and spices he couldn't identify. But it was the quiet sobs tearing out of the woman's chest that broke his heart.

"What's wrong? Did something else happen?" *Don't let her water have broken.* Unheroic or not, he grimaced at the thought of what that would do to his leather seats.

She raised her head and stared at him in surprise, her long lashes spiky with tears. "Y-you came back?"

Back? Humbled, he leaned a shoulder against the roof and reached out to wipe the tears off the cheek closest to him, noting the unbelievable softness of her skin. "Sweetheart, I wouldn't leave you here like this. I had to turn around and I didn't want to do it with you in the car in case I ran off the road."

The woman touched her tongue to her lips, wetting them. What he could see of her expression looked to be a mixture of disbelief, thankfulness and fear.

The stress of the day left him in that instant—work, family problems, the snow and the ridiculously expensive seats. Staring into her tear-streaked face he bit back his questions and anger as to why she was alone, and forced himself to smile. "Tell you what," he told her, grateful his head was being spared the biting shards of ice since he'd ducked beneath the car roof, "I'll forgive you for not believing in me if you'll tell me your name. Deal?"

She laughed abruptly, the gust of sound tear choked and rough. "D-deal." She gave him a wobbly smile, her cheek moving against his hand. "I'm Darcy, Darcy Rhodes."

"Garret Tulane." He dropped his palm from her face and took her fingers in his, squeezing gently. "Nice to meet you, Darcy." Shaking once, he let go but didn't move away. "You're not alone, okay? Not anymore. But we do have a major problem."

Darcy's brave face crumpled for a moment before she pulled herself together with a deep inhalation and a courageous nod. She looked down at her stomach, her hands roaming over the mound in rapid strokes indicative of her state of mind.

"You don't have a cell signal, either, do you?"

"No, but I do have OnStar and I contacted the hospital. It's small and they don't have an ambulance available right now. Which means even though I'm a stranger, you're going to have to trust me enough to let me drive you there. Think you can do that?"

Fresh tears flooded her eyes, but she blinked rapidly and not a single drop fell. "I don't know where it is."

"Then you're in luck." Admiring her spunk, he bent lower and reached across her to unbuckle her seat belt. "Because I know exactly where it is. I work at the hospital and I could find it in my sleep. You'll be well cared for."

"You're a doctor?"

He saw hope flare in her eyes and hated to disappoint her. "No, but—" A firm little *whack* hit his arm where his coat had pulled back from his wrist. He glanced down in surprise. "Whoa."

Darcy snorted. "Kicks like a soccer player," she informed him, her expression sad and proud at the same time. "But it's too soon. I can't have the baby now because it's *too soon.*"

He stomped down his own fears of what the next hour or so might bring and tried to adopt a reassuring expression. "Hey, stress is only going to make things worse, right? So you can't stress," he ordered gently. "Try to relax and let me get you to the hospital. Concentrate on staying calm."

She sniffled but nodded, then took a deep, shuddering breath. "Hear that, Cameron? We need to destress. Garret is going to take us to the hospital, and you're going to stay put—that's an order."

He noted the way her stroking hands had slowed their frantic pace. "Good job." Once more he leaned over her, pressed the release on the seat belt and then pulled it loose. "Grab your purse and I'll help you. Be careful of the ice."

Darcy gripped his arm and held, her face a scant inch away from his. "My suitcase. Will you get it? I want my things, the baby's things. Just in case. It's in the trunk. Please?"

Garret bit back his impatience, but if he'd learned nothing else in his years working at the hospital, it was to not mess with hormonal, expectant mothers. "I'll take care of it. But let's get you settled first and strapped in, okay?" He braced himself while she shifted to get out. "Careful. That's it, I've got you." He wrapped an arm around her waist and held on while she walked the few steps it took to get her to the Escalade. Her foot slipped on the running board getting in.

Time slowed in that split second. Her foot slipped, Darcy gasped, and he wrapped his arms around her so that her weight fell against him, praying she'd land on him and not the ice. Somehow he managed to keep them both on their feet, his nose landing in her hair from where it spilled beneath a knit cap. Heart thumping wildly, they stood frozen for several long seconds. Finally Garret squeezed her gently to let her know she was safe, and urged her inside.

Grabbing the seat belt, he pulled it out for her to take and got another whiff of evergreen. He'd thought it was an air freshener inside her car, but the smell was too strong. Her perfume? Whatever it was, the scent was natural and earthy and completely unlike the heavy, designer fragrances Jocelyn favored.

The multiple lights over her head and from the dash were brighter than the single one in her small car, giving Garret his first good look at her.

A riot of soft blond curls tangled around Darcy's tear-streaked face. She had a small, straight nose—

albeit red and runny—and what looked to be chocolate-brown eyes. But it was her full, wide mouth that held his attention. While she fumbled to latch the seat belt, she sank her teeth into the soft pink flesh of her trembling lower lip. He stared, transfixed until a blast of wind nearly knocked him off his feet, reminding him that now was not the time to be standing around.

Garret shook his head at himself and went for her suitcase, stowed it in the backseat of the SUV before climbing in beside her just in time to see Darcy's face tighten with the onset of another contraction.

"Garret?"

"Yeah, sweetheart?"

"Um…I think we'd better hurry."

DARCY HATED putting more pressure on her rescuer, but she was scared out of her mind. And with every contraction her fears quadrupled. She still had six weeks to go, so now was too early for this baby to arrive.

The vehicle slipped and slid, and maneuvering the ice-coated road required Garret's undivided attention. A good thing, considering how self-conscious she felt about having groaning, hug-the-belly pains in front of a gorgeous stranger. What if he had to deliver her baby?

Times like these called for her to be pragmatic but

she hadn't shaved her legs and had worn her most comfortable panties. She didn't want her handsome driver to remember her due to the holes in her underwear. Wouldn't that be a story for his grandkids?

"How far is it?" she asked when the contraction was over and the silence in the vehicle became too much. "Are we close?"

"Very. Just relax."

"Why don't I believe you?"

Garret smiled, his teeth looking impossibly white. Why couldn't she have been rescued by a sweet little old midwife?

"Because you're too perceptive for your own good? The hospital isn't far, less than ten or fifteen minutes on a good day."

But what about a really bad one? "If the baby comes—"

"It won't."

"But if it *does* and you have to deliver it," she continued determinedly, her face growing hot. "I just want to apologize in advance." *For the underwear, the porcupine legs and the mess and trauma birth would cause the immaculate vehicle and you,* she added silently.

She shouldn't have waited so late in her pregnancy to move. She should have known Stephen would never come around and man up to being a dad. She should have moved months ago. In fall, not winter!

"Nothing's going to happen to you or the baby. And there's no need to apologize. You're getting yourself worked up because you're scared. Sit back and relax. Think happy thoughts."

Was he kidding? She closed her eyes and leaned her head against the buttery-soft seat. "I should've been more responsible and stopped for the night before it got dark. Then I wouldn't have made the stupid wrong turn."

"The weather front shifted suddenly. You couldn't have known. Besides, I don't know a single woman who wouldn't be frightened right now. But you've got to remember that stress isn't good for the baby. You're doing fine, Darcy. Just try to stop giving yourself such a hard time."

Easy for him to say. She could mentally kick herself all the way to Canada and not be satisfied. The move, the weather. And she couldn't have spared five minutes to shave her legs? "Do you do that for a living? Give pep talks?"

Garret chuckled, the sound gravelly and soothing at the same time. "I push paper and placate temper tantrums more often than not. But sometimes pep talks are needed, too, so yeah."

He looked the type. Sort of like the old gentlemen farmers, all proper manners and clothes on the surface, but calloused and hard beneath. "Then I guess I'll listen to you. I mean I'm trying…" Her words trailed to a stop and she shook her head, unable to give voice to the horrible images rumbling through her brain.

What if the baby came? Would it live?

The void of their conversation was broken by the swoosh of the wipers, the heater fan blowing full blast and the crunch of the ice and snow beneath the tires. The SUV slid as they headed into a curve, and she gasped and braced herself to take a bite out of another guardrail. But other than lurching to one side, the big vehicle kept its course, and Garret's cool thinking and reflexes allowed him to maintain control.

He shot her an apologetic glance. "Sorry about that. You okay?"

She nodded, unnerved by the second close call. "It happens fast, doesn't it?"

"Yeah, especially in the mountains. I saw your tags when I turned around. You're from Florida?"

"Miami. I...I've lived in Miami the past four years." No sooner had the words left her mouth than the pain returned. She stiffened in the seat, trying hard to keep quiet. How could something that lasted mere seconds hurt so much?

When it was over, she couldn't stop shaking. "It's too quiet," she whispered abruptly.

"What kind of music do you like?"

"No, not— I...I need words. Music doesn't distract me b-because I can tune it out. Talk to me.

I know you need to concentrate, but I keep thinking about all the things that could happen and— Tell me something. Anything. Recite the alphabet if you want to, I don't care. You said you work at the hospital? What do you do?"

Garret could probably feel her desperation, certainly hear it in her voice. While she'd like to have kept a cool head, it simply wasn't possible. What if she had this all wrong? What if something happened to her and the baby survived? What then?

Her stomach threatened to heave at her thoughts. *Stop this. Stop thinking worst-case scenario.*

"I'm the administrative chief of staff at the hospital. It's basically a fancy title for a job that means I make sure the hospital runs smoothly. Contract negotiating, staffing, supplies, security. It all falls under a big umbrella that I oversee."

She lifted a hand to shove her hair off her face. "That sounds hectic."

"It can be. But it leaves the doctors and nurses to concentrate on what they do best."

"Another power player." Anger surfaced out of nowhere. Stephen had loved the authority that came with people reporting to him—especially the maids, although she hadn't found that out until after they'd broken up. Realizing she'd said the words aloud, she faltered. "Sorry. No offense."

"I don't take offense easily."

"I only meant that with a job like that you must enjoy… being in charge."

"I still have to report to the president and the board, but who doesn't like a little say-so in some way or another?" He shrugged. "One of my brothers refers to me as the gatekeeper."

A wave of heat swept over her and her heart picked up speed. Steadily increasing pressure tightened her muscles and gathered around her middle. "Is the nickname…appropriate?" *Don't think about the contractions. They're nothing. They don't—*

She must have made some noise because Garret's hands rotated on the steering wheel, like he wanted to twist and grind it into nothing. The sight touched her more than words could. If he could take the pain away, do something to help her, she knew without a doubt he would. How sweet was that?

"I guess I could be called a scaled-back adrenaline junkie. I get my kicks from solving problems in high-stress situations."

"You must be loving this, then."

He reached over the console and placed his hand on her forearm. "No man likes seeing a woman in pain. Hang in there, we're getting closer."

She tried to smile but couldn't. They might be getting closer, but so were the contractions.

CHAPTER THREE

"Focus, Darcy. Don't think about the pain or worry about what's not going to happen. What did you do in Miami? Huh? Sweetheart, talk to me."

Darcy supposed the situation called for a get-to-know-you info dump because if the baby decided to make its debut, he'd get to know her a *lot* better sooner rather than later. He should probably know a few things about her before discovering she preferred hi-cut low riders over the thongs she'd set aside at five months.

"I worked for a couple of privately owned hotels, before that a gym and a hotel chain." She hesitated, glimpsed his expectant expression for her to fill in the blanks and sighed. "I'm an aromatherapist. I use scented oils in massage therapy."

She waited, really not in the mood for a snarky comment about her profession. Would he be like other people? Look at her, her belly, and smirk?

"Are you having another contraction?"

He probably thought so because of the way she

was grinding her teeth, but grasping the excuse, she closed her eyes and leaned her head against the seat. Let him think what he wanted. She knew all guys weren't hound dogs, but her experience working in Miami was that *most* guys who dressed like Garret and drove vehicles like this equated her profession to prostitution. Toss in her pregnant, unmarried state and— Well, most men assumed that she'd played sex games with one too many of her clients and was now paying the price.

You're awfully sensitive, there. This guy hasn't said a word.

But how long would it be until he did? Stephen's parents, and Stephen himself, had had plenty to say about the pregnancy. They'd gotten down and dirty in the insult department when she'd refused to do their bidding and abort.

"Have you ever seen snow?"

She wet her lips, relaxing slightly. *Thanks for sending me a gentleman, Nana.* "I'm originally from southern Indiana, so yeah, I've seen snow."

"And you said you're moving back there? How'd an Indiana girl wind up in Miami?"

Darcy nibbled her lower lip, her gaze on her hands as they moved over her stomach. "The Indiana girl thought Miami was warm and a great change of pace."

Another contraction consumed her, heat first,

then pain, harder than any of the others. She leaned forward, balling up in an attempt to fight it.

"Easy. Try to breathe."

"*C-can't.*"

"Yes, you can." He put her hand on her back, rubbing gently. "Come on, Darcy. Listen to my voice. Breathe out, slowly. Good. Now inhale."

When it was over, she straightened and glared at him. A man should have to experience childbirth. *Don't be so cocky,* you *haven't experienced it yet.* "Are we close? Please, tell me we're close."

"Getting there. Beauty is a great little town," he added, pride lacing his voice. "Very low crime, everybody knows each other. I went away to college, but moved back once I graduated because I missed it so much. Some guys want to travel the world, but I knew all along I wanted to stay close to my roots. Wait until you see it and you'll understand what I mean."

"It sounds nice. I—I want that for my baby. Roots and stability. That's why I'm moving back home." But it wasn't home. It hadn't felt like home even when she lived there. Was she doing the right thing?

"Families are good to have around, especially when there are kids involved. I have three brothers and a sister, plus the parents and a huge assortment of aunts, uncles and cousins."

One aspect of his story stuck out in her mind. "Your mother went through this *five* times?"

Garret chuckled, the sound a smooth bass. "Four, actually. My younger brothers are twins."

At the mention of his brothers, his expression grew... mournful? Whatever it was, something in his tone kept her from asking for more details, much as she wanted to. She was curious by nature and having no real family of her own, she loved hearing about other people's.

That was the best part of her job. Facedown on the table, some of her clients habitually unloaded their family problems as though she were a shrink. She knew the names of children, grandchildren. Pets. She'd learned when to ask questions and when to keep quiet and let them ramble.

Garret wasn't rambling. "Is the, um, hospital a good one? Nice people and all? And the baby unit? Are they good with preemies?"

Once again he reached over and squeezed her arm. She felt the heat of his touch through her coat and appreciated the comfort it brought. She wasn't her mother. She didn't hang all over men trying to get them to notice her. If anything she kept her distance and waited them out. But Garret's frequent caresses weren't creepy or touchy-feely, just...nice.

"You're not going to have a preemie. We're going

to get there and they're going to stop the contractions. We're not far, but I have to go slow or risk driving us over the side of the mountain."

"I know." She rubbed her aching head with her free hand. "I couldn't believe it when I started to slide. I was going *so* slow, but— My car's really screwed up. It wouldn't start after I crashed and I don't know where to get it fixed or when I'll be able to get back on the road. What if they can't stop the labor? What if the baby has to stay in the hospital for a while? I need to get settled in Indiana, find a job and get an apartment, but…I could be a mom tonight."

Or not.

Chills racked her. The baby had to survive. Be okay. But if they couldn't stop the labor and it *was* born tonight— Was she ready for this? The crying and feeding and supporting, *raising*. And later? If she managed to do all those things, no way was her baby going to drive at fifteen. And dating? Yeah, right. Samuel Tolbert had tried to feel her up at that age—and go a lot further. She'd kneed him in the nuts and walked home. No way would her son or daughter be anywhere near the opposite sex before they were twenty—at least!

"I can recommend a great mechanic. There's nothing he can't fix, so you don't have to worry about that."

She made a face. "Hate to tell you this, but if you drive this kind of vehicle and are still going to the shop a lot for him to fix things, your mechanic is a crook."

Another chuckle. The man would make a fortune bottling the sound.

"Not Nick. He's my brother and a good guy."

There it was again. That tone of his was...sad. "Why do you say it like that?"

While he remained staring straight ahead Garret's expression changed to one she couldn't read. "Like what?"

"If he's a good guy, why do you sound sad about it?"

"I guess because the family doesn't see much of Nick even though he owns the garage in town."

"Should I ask why you don't see him...or keep my mouth shut?"

"It's complicated."

She squirmed, unable to get comfortable. Her back was killing her. "You two have a big fight over a girl?" Tension crept in, slow and sure, wrapping around her like a python, squeezing, *squeezing*, until she couldn't breathe.

"It was nothing like that. Long story short, Nick went against the family wishes and dropped out of high school. Our parents, grandparents—everyone got involved from teachers to the guy at the feed store. And the more people talked, the more distanced and angry Nick became. Things have been tense ever since."

"How long ago…was this?" She gritted her teeth and fought to focus on Garret instead of the pain.

"About fifteen years."

"And they're—*oh*—still upset?" She gasped out the words.

The Escalade slid to the left as they started across a bridge, and Garret slowed even more. She wanted to scream at him to go faster, but couldn't take a breath.

Shaking, unable to fight the tears or the pain any longer and pretend she could do this with dignity, she released a low groan. "G-Garret?"

"Yeah?"

"I don't think we're going to make it."

GARRET GLANCED at his watch when the contraction finally released its hold. That one had lasted forty-two seconds. No way could he deliver a baby. A legal brief he could handle. A crisis involving multiple unions—a friggin' walk in the park. But a *baby?*

Over the crunching precipitation, he heard Darcy moan, and glanced over to see relief etched on her pale, strained features. "Good one?"

"Oh, yeah."

There were tears in her voice, one trickling down her cheek. Considering they were still miles away from the hospital, the sound and sight sent chills through him. Twenty miles an hour on a winding mountain road was getting them nowhere fast.

"Go on," she murmured. "Please, tell me the story about your brother. It helps to focus on someone else."

He looked at the road ahead of him, not liking the subject but willing to go along with the request. Whatever it took to get both their minds off the present predicament. "Nick dropped out as soon as he didn't need our parents' permission. They were disappointed and upset, and when they couldn't get Nick to do what they wanted, they looked to me to get Nick to change his mind."

"Why you?"

"I'm older than him and a good negotiator. Even as a kid, I settled the arguments in my family." He smiled wryly, various scenes popping into his head. "I actually used to hold court about my siblings' disputes. I'd hear the sides and make a judgment on everything from whose box of crayons it really was to who got to ride in the front seat. But this fight— It was huge. In the end Dad got frustrated and lost his temper. He and Nick are a lot alike that way. Dad told Nick he either had to stay in school or get out of the house."

"The perfect words to make a teenager rebel."

"Exactly. So Nick left. He moved out and lived in a storage area above our uncle's garage."

"Poor guy."

He found himself chuckling at Darcy's description, glad to have something to smile about. "Poor, he's not. Nick's done really well for himself. My uncle owns a variety of businesses around town and he gave Nick a job in his garage."

"Then he's okay?"

She was worried about Nick? Garret nodded to reassure her, liking her compassion. How many people in her situation would be thinking of someone else? "He's done better than okay. A few years later Uncle Cyrus had a heart attack and couldn't work for a while. Nick stepped up to the plate and ran the garage on his own." He flashed her a grin. "Picture an eighteen-year-old kid bossing around mechanics two and three times his age—and getting away with it."

"Your uncle didn't mind?"

"Nah, Uncle C. was so impressed by all the compliments about Nick's work and business ethic that he sold out to Nick when he retired. That's why I said Nick's not a crook. He's had years to take advantage of people if he wanted, but I've never once heard someone say that he's ripped them off."

"Sounds like your brother deserves all the praise after working so hard."

"I think so. He bought the building beside the garage not long ago. It was a gym he went to until the owner started going under because of poor management and rumors of cameras in the women's locker room."

"Pervert. So Nick's a real entrepreneur."

"Yeah, despite his lack of education, turns out he's a great businessman. He's a pretty good dad, too."

Normally he wouldn't dream of discussing Nick and his family's situation with an outsider. Garret couldn't remember ever really discussing it with Jocelyn, but something about Darcy made him feel comfortable. She wasn't judgmental; instead she was supportive, acting as though she could relate.

"He's doing all of that and raising a child?"

Garrett nodded. "He's got one kid. My nephew."

"Good for him. He showed the family, didn't he? He struck out on his own and did well, all the while being a dad. That's admirable."

Darcy was obviously a compassionate person, but when she spoke it was as though Nick's achievements were her own. Because she dreamed of doing the same thing herself? Striking out and being a success while raising her baby? While Garrett applauded independence, he couldn't help but wonder where the baby's father was.

Politically correct or not, what kind of man allowed the mother of his child to travel so far alone? He'd noticed her lack of wedding band. How upset would she be if he asked?

It's none of your business.

"You should be proud of him."

He *was* proud of Nick. Once his little brother had gotten away from the family, Nick's confidence and abilities had soared. There was something significant in that.

Garret turned onto the more heavily traveled road leading to Beauty, thankful the salt trucks had already been there. He still couldn't race to get his passenger to the hospital, but he was able to pick up speed. This close, he wouldn't have to deliver anything but Darcy into the welcoming hospital doors. "I don't want to leave you with a bad impression of my family. They're great, and they love Nick. All of us do. Things simply got out of hand and snowballed."

"That's a *really* bad joke given the weather." Her breathing picked up as another contraction hit.

He glanced at her repeatedly, wishing he could do more to help.

"Families d-don't always get along, but th-they should stay close. Don't you think?"

"Yeah, I do. But what about you? Would you like me to call someone for you? The baby's father?"

Her curls stuck to her cheek when she shook her head. "No."

Hurt, anger. Regret or sadness. The multilayered emotions flickered over her face before Darcy's features smoothed into one of grim determination.

"I'm sorry, Darcy. You would've asked if you wanted my help. That's none of my business."

"It's okay. Obviously if I'm in the middle of Tennessee alone, there's a problem, right?" Her mouth turned down at the corners. "The father and I aren't together. He signed away his rights so I would leave him alone. This baby is entirely mine."

Silence followed her words, but he could've sworn he heard her whisper, *If it makes it.*

Knowing she had every right to be worried and angry at the idiot who'd take advantage of her, he grasped her hand, holding it loosely.

After a moment, a sniffle; her fingers tightened around his. "Garret?"

"Yeah?"

"Are we there yet?"

CHAPTER FOUR

NOT LONG AFTER she'd asked the age-old question in an attempt to lighten the intensity of the moment and the effect Garret holding her hand had on her emotions—who knew holding hands could feel so good?—they pulled beneath the hospital's canopied E.R. entrance. He hurried out of the Cadillac to get help.

Darcy watched as he disappeared inside the double doors, sending up a prayer of thanks because they'd made it safely. She'd been found, and not by a knife-wielding psycho.

The doors slid open again and Garret emerged with several smocked individuals. Within moments she was placed in a wheelchair and whisked inside. Her last glimpse of Garret was as he stood beneath the harsh outdoor lights talking with someone, his dark hair and long wool coat very dramatic against the snowy backdrop.

"When are you due?" an aide asked.

"Mid-March. I've got s-six weeks left." They rushed by the waiting area and veered left.

"Have you had any problems before now?"

Forcing herself to focus on one problem at a time, she nodded reluctantly. "Cramping, if I overdid things. But my doctor in Florida ran some tests and said everything was normal."

The woman wheeled her into an elevator that soared to the second floor with stomach-jarring swiftness, and off they went again. Darcy saw a Labor and Delivery sign posted above a set of doors and after keying in a code, the aide pushed Darcy through as another contraction hit.

"Almost there, honey."

She wheeled Darcy into a room and then disappeared, leaving her in the hands of two waiting nurses. The contraction ended and they helped her step out of the wheelchair. While one nurse went to work on removing Darcy's coat, the second nurse shut the door and snagged a cart from its position near a wall, pushing it toward the bed. It was loaded down with supplies and a machine that looked like something off a space ship.

"What's that?" Darcy asked, wishing absurdly that Garret had accompanied her. She could've used a hand to hold.

"Don't worry about anything, hon," the older of the two nurses said. "We're going to get you in a gown and then we're going to start you on some fluids. After that, we'll hook you up to a monitor to get a reading on the baby's heartbeat, and find out what's going on. I'm Betty," the woman added, "and this is Debra. If you need anything and we're not in here, you press that call button right there on the bed. But don't get up, and don't mess with these machines. If something slips or moves, you call us. Got it?"

Darcy nodded dazedly.

"Good. Now let's get you settled in and all hooked up."

She begged a trip to the bathroom, hoping the act would ease the cramping. It didn't. When she emerged, the nurses helped her out of her blouse and propped her against the bed as another contraction built in intensity. While she breathed through it, they stripped her down, guiding her arms into a gown and snapping it closed with minimal fuss. Their impersonal attitude allowed her to set aside her embarrassment over her hairy legs and ratty underwear.

At least Garret's not seeing it.

The nurses wrapped straps around Darcy's stomach, inserted an IV into her arm with surprising gentleness and fired so many questions at her she could barely answer one before the next query came. Finally the nurse who'd been prepping her with needles, blood pressure cuffs and monitors stood back and checked her handiwork.

Betty finished taking notes in the chart, then smiled. "We're all set. Debra and I are going to check on our other patients, but we'll watch the monitors from the desk. You just lie there and relax. Mr. Tulane specifically asked for Dr. Clyde, and you're in luck because she's still here. She's in delivery right now, but soon as she's done, you'll meet her."

"Where's…Mr. Tulane?" She'd almost referred to him as Garret, but here and now the closeness she felt after the rescue didn't seem appropriate.

"I have no idea. You must have been so frightened. Were you stuck out there long?"

She wasn't sure. "A while."

"Well, we'll take good care of you. Don't worry about anything."

She knew they needed to go, that they had other patients to tend to, but she didn't want to be alone. "Wait—please." She made herself meet their gazes. "Am I going to lose my baby?"

Both nurses fussed and smiled at her before they left to get someone to help her with the necessary paperwork. But neither of them answered her question.

When they were gone, Darcy wrapped her arms around her belly and held tight, ignoring the pull of the tape holding her IV in place.

Stephen had gone on and on about how people like them weren't meant to be parents.

Please, God, don't let him be right.

"Don't you ever leave?"

Garret looked up from his desk to see Tobias Richardson standing in the doorway. Turning so that Toby could see the phone he held pressed to his ear, Garret reluctantly waved his friend in and tried to push through his distraction to concentrate on the hospital president's words.

But every time he closed his eyes he remembered the look on Darcy's face, the feel of her fingers holding on to his. It had only been a moment, several minutes at most, but something about it had gotten to him.

"I want something done and I want it done *now.*"

Harold Pierson growled the words into Garret's ear and jerked him from his thoughts. His boss wasn't a patient man, and the fact it was midnight on a Friday only seemed to increase Harry's insistence that his demands be met.

Garret rubbed his forehead, pen in hand. "I spoke with maintenance before I called. The problem's been taken care of."

"You're sure?"

If Harry would leave well enough alone, then yeah, Garret was sure. "Yes. I also had the men double-check the generators and the salt supplies. Everything's taken care of. Trust me on this and try to enjoy your weekend." *So I can enjoy mine.*

"What about the meeting Monday morning? Are those idiots still driving down from Nashville?"

As of January first, Beauty Medical Center had become a branch location for a much larger university hospital based in Nashville. According to Harry, the merger was the death knell of all they held dear. Garret knew enough to keep his mouth shut about his belief that the change was the best thing to happen to the town and the hospital. "I'll contact you once I know the meeting's status."

"Are you spending the night to keep an eye on things?"

He didn't doubt Harry would like for him to do just that. But having put in nearly eighty hours this week, the last thing Garret wanted to do was sleep here. Bad enough he hadn't gotten any work done until after Harry had left. Once he knew Darcy was okay and the roads had another layer of salt on them, he was out of here. "If there's a problem, I'll handle it over the phone or drive back in."

Toby grunted at his statement, and Garret shot him a warning glare. Garret did *not* need Harry to overhear Toby's mutters. Harry didn't like Toby for the sole reason that he thought Toby had overstepped his humble upbringing by becoming an attorney.

Well, that and the lawn incident. Twenty years ago Toby's mom—Harry's housekeeper for a very brief period of time—had arranged for her son to mow Harry's lawn. He had watched Toby the entire six hours required to mow and weed the yard. When Toby had finished, Harry had refused to pay because he claimed Toby had done it wrong. In retaliation, Toby had dumped the day's accumulation of grass clippings in the pool.

"If that SOB in maintenance spouts his nonsense again—"

"I've taken care of everything." Garret opened the desk drawer and searched through the Tums, Alka-Seltzer and peppermints for something to ease his pounding head.

"Fine, then. You take care of things but keep me posted. I'm counting on you, Garret."

"I know, sir. I won't let you down."

Toby grunted again. "Suck up."

"You're a good man," Harry said. "Jocelyn complained the other day that I'm working you too hard, but I assured her you were only doing your job."

Garret concentrated on Harry's first comment and ignored the second. He was doing his job plus the majority of Harry's. Over the years Harry had piled more and more on Garret's shoulders. Now Harry had a damn good golf swing and Garret practically ran this place without receiving any credit.

Don't get too big for your britches. You do that and you'll end up going naked cause nothin' fits your ego.

Garret pinched the bridge of his nose, a smile

pulling at one side of his mouth. Man, he missed Grandpa. "I'll be sure to call Joss tomorrow."

"You do that. She's been working quite a bit herself lately. Her mother thinks it's because she's lonely and missing you with all the hours you're putting in on the merger. But I'm thinking it's something else entirely."

"Something else, sir?" He ignored Toby's impatient glance at his watch. "Is something wrong?"

"Nothing you can't fix. Did you know I proposed to my Charlotte on Valentine's Day? This year will be twenty-nine years. The date's creeping up, you know."

The hint wasn't subtle. Neither were any of the others Harold had dropped over the past year. "I believe you've mentioned that."

Harry's booming voice had to be carrying to Toby's ears. Garret swung sideways in the office chair in a poor attempt to gain some privacy.

"I suspect you'll do right by our girl then. Soon."

"Of course, sir. If there's nothing else, I'll talk to you tomorrow. I've got a few things to take care of before I head home."

"Fine, fine. Go take care of business. When you talk to maintenance again, tell them I expect hospital property to be clear at all times, and that idiot—"

"Understood," Garret said before Harry could go off on another tangent about the Maintenance Department's performance. The team was top-notch, but Harry wasn't satisfied. "Good night, sir." Garret dropped the phone and held up a hand when Toby immediately opened his mouth. "Don't—"

"Comment on that? Yeah, right. The Whipping Boy's getting an earful tonight. What's got the old goat's goat?"

Garret glared at his friend and returned to his search of the drawer. Finding what he wanted, he pulled out some ibuprofen and downed two with the help of lukewarm root beer left over from lunch twelve hours earlier. He grimaced at the flat taste. "What are you doing here?"

"I was wondering the same thing about you." Toby nodded toward the door. "Maria's in labor and Rob's trying to get back from a business trip in this mess so I got elected to drive her and Ma. Labor and Delivery is a busy place tonight."

"Always is when the barometric pressure drops or there's a full moon. Freaky stuff," Garret muttered, referring to all the cyclical and otherwise unexplainable things that happened in a hospital. He'd learned to prepare for these events over the years after being caught off guard the first year or so on the job. Weather changes were nearly as busy as holidays when families turned against each other and the world's most inept chefs decided they wanted to be Emeril and speed chop.

"You can say that again." Toby's agreement was

packed with the vehemence of a confirmed bachelor. "I grabbed this on the way out, thinking I'd slip it under your door." He lifted the file and waved it in the air for a few seconds to make his point before dropping it onto the desk. "The Jacobs settled and agreed to no press statements or public discussions regarding the case. Signed and sealed."

"Thank God." Garret rubbed his hands over his face in an attempt to ease the tension and fatigue. At least that was one problem handled with minimal fuss. The doctor at fault had been ordered to seek employment elsewhere months ago. But keeping the hospital's name out of the papers because of a surgical accident hadn't been easy. Or cheap.

"You know," Toby said, "we could always go through with our plan from law school."

"Beauty would never be the same with the two of us in practice together."

"Just an option to think about. Gotta admit we'd set the white shoe boys on their asses if we did."

Garret nodded as he always did whenever Toby brought the subject of a partnership up, and added the file to the stack he would take home with him—a stack to match the one already in his SUV from his first attempt to leave. He needed to review the settlement before passing the news on to the board at the meeting Monday morning. If there *was* a meeting. Having to reschedule would screw up a whole week's worth of meetings. Was that what life was about? A series of meetings? Was he destined to spend his days listening to Harry complain?

Toby's reminder about their law school ideas left Garret scowling. He'd like to say that opening a practice had been the pipe dream of two idealistic attorneys out to change the world, but that wasn't true.

"You look like hell. Bad day?"

"You could say that." Garret stacked the piles together and stuffed them into his briefcase. He'd told the nurses to call him if things took a turn for the worse and they weren't going to be able to stop Darcy's labor. Did that mean they had? He should've instructed them to update him no matter what.

"I heard that trip to Nashville yesterday scored you a nice ride."

He grimaced. News traveled fast. It had been Harry's responsibility to go to Nashville, but the president had balked at the last minute with a bogus excuse, sending Garret to deal with the university hospital officials instead. Knowing he'd come back to a disaster after a single day away, the visit to the car lot had been a gift to himself. "Always wanted a convertible. It'll be delivered this spring in time for the pretty weather."

He stood and pulled on his coat, piled more files into the already-full briefcase and led the way to the door. Another week gone in the blink of an eye. It wouldn't be so bad if he didn't leave his house before six every morning to hit the gym and arrive at work before the sun did more than brighten the horizon. Why buy a convertible if he could only drive it in the dark? "You'll love it when we take it to the course for the charity golf tournament in June."

Toby waited while Garret locked the office. "Like that'll happen. You'll cancel again. What was it last time? Something to do with the nurses' union?"

"Security upgrade," Garret corrected automatically, his brain clicking through time and events by the problems that had crept up and ruined his enjoyment of them. Toby had a point there, as much as Garret hated to acknowledge it. The odds were against him. "The new system kept going off every five minutes, and it was upsetting all the parents with infants in the nursery." He lifted the leather case and used the worn corner to punch the down arrow at the elevator. "You'll thank me once your niece is in there and all is quiet."

"That law degree must really help with handling that kind of stuff."

Garret twisted his neck, sighing in relief when it popped loudly. "Enough, Tobe. My job may not be one hundred percent law—"

"Or even twenty."

"—but I'm good at what I do and—"

"Your father and grandfather worked hard to get

you the position," Toby muttered, his voice reeking of boredom as he made the statement. "Hey, I get that there are perks, and I know guys who'd kill for your pay. But for all the hours and headaches I don't see much in it for you besides a ridiculous salary and a prime parking space. Is the money worth all… that?" He indicated the bulging briefcase.

"Everything's going to be shut down because of the snowstorm. Joss and I are supposed to get together this weekend, but with the snow I thought maybe we could stay in and—"

"Work?" Toby smirked.

"Back off, Tobe. Not now, okay?"

His friend looked away, an apologetic expression on his face. "Sorry."

Knowing he should quit while Toby seemed prepared to drop the subject, Garret sighed. "But?"

Toby hesitated a long time. "But," he drawled slowly, "I think it would take a saint to put up with your plans for a snowy weekend." He grinned. "What happened to 'Bare-it Garret?'"

"It was *initiation.*"

"Yeah, well, I still can't believe you wanted to be a part of those drunken idiots."

"Lesson learned. Can we move on? If you've got something to say, spit it out."

"This is perfect weather to get stranded with a beautiful woman. Yet you're planning to *work* for the next forty-eight hours? Give me a break. I'm stuck here, but what's your excuse? When was the last time you spent the weekend in bed with Jocelyn?"

CHAPTER FIVE

GARRET SCOWLED at his friend. "This isn't the high school locker room." He was prepared to deflect the issue rather than acknowledge that Toby was right.

"I'm not asking for details, just trying to make a point."

"Which is that I should take Joss to bed?"

"Yes. No!" Toby shut his eyes and ran a hand through his hair in frustration. "It's just every time I call or see you, you're *here*. It's gotta be hard to have a relationship that way."

The elevator chimed and the doors slid open. Garret stepped on, thankful it was empty. It had been a long, hard week and he was too exhausted to examine his life. That would require brain power he didn't have. He wanted to check on Darcy's condition and make sure she'd stabilized, drive home and go to sleep, all without having to process or think.

"Look, the fact that you're not saying anything

says you know I'm on to something." Toby followed Garret into the elevator and punched the button for the cafeteria level.

"You're not on to anything. I'm humoring you by not arguing." Garret punched the L&D floor and hoped his friend wouldn't notice.

"You forget where you parked?"

"I have to stop by the nurses' station and check on something." If he told Toby the truth, his friend would go off on another tangent about how Garret went overboard when it came to his job. To some, simply bringing Darcy in meant his Good Samaritan deed was done. But to him a visit was the least he could do. She was all alone, scared. His right hand curled with the memory of her hand clutching his.

Toby remained quiet, but Garret was aware of his scrutiny the entire time. The elevator chimed and the doors opened once more.

"Remember Michelle?"

He'd known Toby wasn't through. "Why?"

"You pretended to be sick halfway through a date because you said she snorted every time she laughed."

"It was annoying as hell."

"But you didn't tell her that. And what was the other one's name? The one with the big boobs? Rachel? Rochelle? She lasted, what, a month? You ended things with her after you caught her not giving the excess change back to the cashier when she'd given her too much."

"The point, Toby?"

"What are you waiting for? You haven't ended things with Jocelyn, but you haven't moved forward, either. You're in a holding pattern."

Garret glanced around to ensure the hallway was clear before he rounded on his friend. "You know, you're beginning to sound like Harry."

Toby shoved his hands into the pockets of his leather coat. "That's low. Can't we have a simple discussion?"

"You're not looking for a discussion, you're looking for a debate, and so help me—"

"Why haven't you popped the question? You bought the ring."

Garret locked his jaw to keep from swearing a blue streak. "Keep your voice down."

Toby shrugged like a man who knew it wasn't *his* bachelorhood on the line.

Garret stepped closer. "What is this about?" The doors started to close and he shoved the briefcase out to hold them open. He told himself to let it go, to drop the discussion and get out of there while he could. But something wouldn't let him. "What is it you're trying so hard not to say?"

Toby's ears turned red, a sure sign his friend was fast losing patience himself. "I already said it. You bought the ring before Christmas—as a *Christmas present*—but the day came and went and you didn't give it to her. I've kept my mouth shut and waited, thinking you'll tell me what the delay's about. You haven't said a word. *What's going on?*"

Garret wasn't sure. Buying Joss the bracelet had been pure impulse and he'd told himself he was going to give it to her in addition to the ring. But when they exchanged gifts… "Nothing's going on, we're fine. The timing was off. And I'm going to do it. I just haven't gotten around to it."

There was that smirk again. Toby had been his friend for too many years. First as schoolmates, then as playmates when Toby's mom had come to work for the Tulanes. Toby knew what buttons to push, and that smirk made Garret want to plant his fist in Toby's mouth.

"Be still my little ol' heart. That's got to be what every woman wants to hear."

Garret fought for patience. He loved Joss, was going to marry her, no doubt about it. Why was Toby hinting otherwise? "Tobe, I don't—" Garret broke off and swore as understanding dawned. "People know? Is that it? Someone else knows besides you and me?" He and Toby had gone to one of the most discreet jewelry stores in Nashville. A high-end business with nondescript signage and an armed guard who met potential customers at the elevator, walked them through a metal detector before escorting them beyond a bullet-proof-glass-partitioned wall to view the merchandise. How had people found out?

"I haven't said anything, but you know how gossip works and that—" he lowered his voice when a woman in scrubs walked by the far end of the hallway "—was a big-ticket item even if it was one of their less expensive rings. How long did you think it would be before people began to speculate?"

"It's none of their business."

"I agree, but I can't blame them when I'm curious, too. She hasn't *mentioned* it?"

"Joss isn't like that."

"Maybe not, but wouldn't she find a way to let you know she's ready even if she didn't come right out and say it? You know, leave bridal magazines lying around? Something?"

The comment gave him pause. Garret forced himself to unlock his jaw so the pain streaking to his head would ease. "Joss is building a career, just like I am. Timing is everything. You've experienced that enough in court, figuring out when to say just the right thing to sway the juries. Joss and I have plenty of time. Marriage isn't something to rush into."

Toby tugged at his ear. "If you say so."

"I do."

"Fine, whatever. If you see Maria or my mother walking the halls, do me a favor and tell them I went to get something to drink. I'll be up in a few minutes."

Subject apparently dropped for now, Garret nodded. "Sure." He pulled the briefcase from the door, but as they slid shut, he was very aware of the fact Toby didn't look any happier than he had when he'd started the strange conversation. His friend meant well, and Garret tried to remember that despite his irritation Toby's questions had hit home. Joss hadn't mentioned getting married since— When? A long time ago, and she'd made the comment so casually he knew she wasn't hinting.

Toby was feeling the pressure every thirtysomething guy out there felt to settle down and do something with his life. Reacting to it. That had to be the reason behind the inquisition. Tobe was freaking out because his sister was on kid number three while he hadn't made it to first base with a woman in months. Parental pressures to reach certain achievements changed as a kid grew older, but they certainly didn't disappear.

Garret walked toward the nurses' station to check on Darcy, each step longer than the last. He eyed the empty area and set his briefcase at his feet, leaning against the desk while he waited for someone to return. Seconds passed, minutes, his thoughts running rampant but finally becoming centered on the one question he couldn't answer.

When *was* the last time he and Joss had had sex?

"WHAT DO YOU MEAN she isn't here?" Five minutes later Garret bit back the curse that sprang to his lips and wiped a hand over his tired eyes. It was one o'clock in the morning and Darcy had been having labor pains. Where else could she be?

The nurse gave him a chilly stare at his tone. "It's hospital policy to treat and release patients provided their condition is under control, Mr. Tulane."

"She didn't drive herself here. Where did she go?"

The older nurse raised her eyebrows and straightened the multitude of charts in front of her by banging the stack against the counter. "I don't know what to tell you, Mr. Tulane, but she's not here. Try the cafeteria or the waiting area by the main entrance. Now I have to go. We're short-staffed tonight." Her tone suggested the situation was his fault.

That was partially true. The nurses' contract was up for renewal and Harold was balking at the pay raise. Not only were the current wages causing them to lose some of their experienced staff, but also the low rates meant new graduates weren't eager to work here when other hospitals paid more. He couldn't blame them.

Scowling, he grabbed his briefcase and turned to

leave, only to stop in his tracks and stare out the nearby window. The hospital appeared to be in the middle of a snow globe. Giant flakes blew in blinding sheets, buffeted by gusts of wind that shook the window in its frame.

Was Darcy out there? Concern overrode every ounce of remaining frustration.

Downstairs, the reception desk was unstaffed, the main lobby empty. The television inside the waiting area was tuned to a local station broadcasting details about the storm he didn't want to consider. Surely she wouldn't have tried to walk? The closest motel was a quarter mile away.

Shaking his head, he hurried to the cafeteria and visually scanned the colorful scrubs and white coats, unease growing when he didn't see her. Where was she?

He'd turned to leave when he spotted her. Darcy sat in the far corner booth with her head propped against her arm. And even though he had no reason to feel the extent of the relief swamping him, he did. Knowing she was all alone and could have easily lost her baby tonight got to him.

Darcy's blond curls were messy and her expression was one of pure exhaustion. But the moment she saw him approach, her brown eyes warmed with welcome. Something twisted inside him at the sight.

She straightened and pushed the small, old-fashioned-looking porcelain doll she'd been staring at into the center of the table. "I was hoping I'd see you again. I didn't get a chance to thank you for all you did for me."

Like kicking her out into the snow? "You're okay?"

She nodded. "Seems so. The contractions were a combination of dehydration and stress. The IVs and medication stopped them almost immediately, and Dr. Clyde said I'm okay. No damage from the accident at all."

"You're not sore?"

She shrugged. "A little in my shoulders and back, but nothing major. Honestly the crash was more like a bumper-car hit because I was going so slow. Taylor and I are fine."

"Taylor? But you called the baby Cameron earlier."

She blushed prettily. "Did I? I like that. I'll have to write that one down."

"Excuse me?"

"I'm trying out names until I find one that fits."

"Okay."

"Don't laugh. How anyone can pick a name out of a book is beyond me. If you really want the truth, I think a parent needs to open the back door and shout it a few times to get the full effect and know if they're going to like hearing it for the next eighteen years or so as they call their kids in for dinner."

This time he laughed outright. "I've never

thought of it quite like that, but you might be on to something."

"Thanks for requesting Dr. Clyde. She's very nice. She wants me to come back if the contractions start again, but otherwise I'm good until my follow-up on Monday."

"I thought she might make you feel more comfortable. She's received good reports during her practice here."

Darcy blinked up at him. "So, what are you still doing here? I would've thought you'd go home after dropping me off."

"I had some things I needed to take care of with the Maintenance Department. I'm heading home now, but I wanted to check on you first."

"That's very sweet. Like I said, I'm fine."

She might be fine, but she looked ready to drop. Inhaling her unique scent, Garret rested the briefcase on top of the table. "You shouldn't have been released in the middle of a storm, not under the circumstances."

"Some rules you can't control. Besides, they did a great job getting the contractions stopped so there's no need to take up a bed. And, being in between jobs like I am at the moment I, uh, don't have a lot of cash to pay for what the insurance doesn't cover. No worries, I promise. They took excellent care of me just like you said they would."

He indicated her suitcase with a nod. "What

happens now? Are you staying in town until your car is fixed?"

Darcy looked down and fingered the doll's satin dress. "I'll be here until the storm is over. But after that I don't know. I'm waiting to hear from my mother. I called but couldn't reach her."

Garret hesitated, knew he should leave well enough alone. "Do you mind if I sit down?"

"Oh, of course. Please do."

He seated himself on the opposite bench. "Are you waiting here for a particular reason?"

She tucked the doll into a cloth sack and put it into her oversize purse. "One of the nurses said if I was still here in the morning, she'd drive me to a motel as soon as her shift was over."

"There isn't another shift change until six. I can't let you sit here for five hours. Come on, you're coming with me."

CHAPTER SIX

Darcy blinked at Garret, surprised by the offer. Go with him where? Finding a place to lie down in the lobby had left her feeling too much like a loser, a *cold* loser, so she'd dragged her achy body to the cafeteria. It was warmer here and she could sleep sitting up, thank you. "I'm okay here."

"No, you're not." Garret stood and grabbed her suitcase with his free hand. "I'll drive you to the motel. It's not far from here."

"You've done enough. More than enou—"

"Darcy? Let me drive you. I'd like to know you're safe."

The words flowed over her, through her, and she found herself fighting back pathetic, exhausted tears. Why not? Debra certainly hadn't acted all that thrilled at the idea of having to take her.

Gazing at him, Darcy absorbed all the little details she'd missed during the dark and pain-shrouded trip to the hospital. Details such as the breadth of Garret's shoulders and the sexy angle of his jawline. She was such a sucker for a strong jawline.

"What do you say? Road trip?"

"Thank you. It's not enough, but thank you—I accept." With a smile of gratitude, Darcy took the arm Garret extended and let him help her to her feet.

Maybe white knights did exist. It was just too bad this one had shown up seven months too late.

GARRET ESCORTED HER to the garage where his SUV was parked.

"Here we are again."

"Here we are," she repeated, buckling her seat belt and watching in amazement when he gently tugged on it to check it. Cinderella she wasn't, but she was sure getting the royal treatment. She'd think he was flirting with her if she wasn't big-as-a-house pregnant. Being that she was, it was easy to rule out romance or anything sexual.

Unlike the pelting ice that had caused her accident, big fluffy flakes the size of marshmallow tops now floated to the ground with deceptive grace and speed. The houses near the hospital were decorated with a mixture of leftover Christmas lights and early Valentine's Day decorations. The older homes were layered with gingerbread trim and pretty porches behind yards with thick tree trunks. The odd swing blew crookedly in the wind.

The farther away from the hospital Garret drove, the more modernized the housing became. Another turn brought them into an area of shops with old-fashioned storefronts. Large, black lampposts stood guard on every corner over benches weighted down with snow, and red fire hydrants poked through drifts to add a splash of color. There was even a striped barber shop sign.

It was the best of Norman Rockwell.

Did the townspeople know how precious this all looked? It was a world apart from the glitz and glamour of Miami. Darcy kept her comments to herself and continued her sleepy study of the little mountain town. Finally Garret braked outside a motel with a cottage-style facade. The Hideaway Inn. *Of course.* She only hoped she could afford it.

"Here we are." He got out and grabbed her suitcase, then escorted her to the door with a solid grip on her arm.

Inside a small anteroom, Darcy shivered and wrinkled her nose at the heavy cinnamon fragrance clouding the air. She loved scents and their healing properties, but this was overkill. No doubt an attempt to diffuse the odor of mold making her nose twitch with a sneeze.

Garret rang the bell attached to the wall. No response. Showing the first signs of impatience, Garret hit the bell a couple more times. Finally a light turned on from the other side of a curtained enclosure beyond the reinforced glass entry doors. A buzz sounded and the small speaker beside the bell squawked.

"Sorry. No rooms."

"The sign says Vacancy." Garret growled the words in his deep, ultrasexy voice, and Darcy felt like the biggest pain in all the world.

"The 'no' is busted and I forgot to turn the darn thing off. Try after the snow lets up." With that suggestion, the light went out and all was silent.

Garret scowled. "Come on. The Station House isn't far. We'll try there."

Back to the vehicle they went and Darcy gasped when the bitter cold hit her face. "I'm sorry for all the trouble."

"It's no problem."

She had to wait until Garret crossed in front of the vehicle and climbed in to continue their conversation. "Just take me back to the hospital. It's fine."

"It's not fine," he murmured firmly. "You need a place to rest. Relax, we'll find you something."

The Station House wound up being a remodeled railroad depot that boasted room service and a restaurant. The cars parked outside were newer models than those of the first motel they'd tried, which meant her credit card would take a harder hit. Still, Garret was right. She was desperate for a place to lie down. She'd never felt this tired, so much so she was starting to nod off beside her handsome driver. How embarrassing. The way her night had gone, she'd fall asleep and drool all over herself.

"Stay here and let me check it out, okay?"

Darcy nodded, willing to let him brave the weather even though she felt guilty for doing so. "Thank you."

Garret flashed her a gorgeous smile and left the vehicle, his shoulders hunched in deference to the cold. She shivered from the influx of cold air and cranked up the heat. It was good of him to let her stay here. A lot of men would worry that the stranger they'd helped would drive off in the expensive Cadi.

She huddled deeper into her seat and frowned at an ad for the radio station's upcoming Valentine's Day contest. There'd be no roses for her this year. No candy or jewelry or candlelight dinners. But that was okay. She'd learned the hard way that flowers and candy didn't make the man. And they most certainly did not make him father material.

Drowsy, she rubbed her belly. "I love you, Annabelle. I hope it's enough."

GARRET SCOWLED at the twentysomething kid in front of him. "You have *nothing* available?"

"Nope."

"I'll make it worth your while. She's pregnant and

stranded and she was just released from the hospital. Don't you have a sitting room or something?"

"No, man. Sorry." The guy grinned, and a crackly laugh emerged. "Weird, huh? You know, no room at the inn?" He sobered when he realized Garret wasn't amused. "Um… look, there's nothing here. This storm caught a lot of people by surprise. We're full and then some." He glanced behind him, then leaned forward across the counter. "We're not supposed to recommend anyplace else, but have you tried the motel on Route 9?"

"Call them," Garret ordered. "Call them right now and find out if there's a room available. Tell them we'll take anything."

The guy gave him a leery, you're-going-to-get-me-in-trouble glare, but did his bidding. Garret paced in front of the counter and blatantly listened to the one-sided conversation. Finally the guy hung up. "Um…nothing, man—uh, sir. Sorry."

Jaw locked, Garret stalked out of the lobby. There wasn't a hotel closet left for Darcy to stay in. Scowling, he climbed into the Escalade only to hesitate when he realized Darcy was sleeping so soundly she hadn't heard him.

He quietly closed the door, free to study her without being observed. She was certainly attractive, but the symmetry of her features was off. Her nose was a little large for her face, her top lip as full as the bottom. Put together, there was nothing awe inspiring about her appearance. Nothing to make him feel so…curious?

He shook his head at himself. Who was it that said if you rescued someone you were responsible for them?

Garret drummed his fingers against the steering wheel. Snow blanketed the windshield despite the frequent swipe of the wipers. They had to get to wherever they were going or be stranded. But there was no way he could leave her sitting in the lobby of some hotel at two o'clock in the morning.

Frowning, he checked her seat belt once more and put the vehicle in Reverse. Someone had to take care of Darcy and her baby. And right now it looked as though that someone was him.

SHE WAS IN A BOAT, sun-warmed air blowing on her face, the chop of the waves slapping against the hull, the radio playing eighties hits by rockers with big hair.

A jolt startled her and Darcy blinked, drowsily surveying her surroundings and wondering why the GPS looked different than she remembered. With a start, it all came back. The wind was a heater cranked full blast, the waves dirt- and sand-encrusted sludge hitting the undercarriage of the SUV.

You expected something else?

Not really. She hadn't been on a boat since the last

time Stephen had taken her out and they'd made love beneath the stars.

You made love, he had sex. Big *difference.*

The SUV slowed for Garret to make a turn. A garage door opened ahead of them and they pulled inside to park beside a Land Cruiser. She lifted her head.

"Hey. You were out the whole way."

"Obviously." The last thing she remembered was sitting outside the Station House. And now they were where? "This doesn't look like a hotel." She eyed the pricey-looking bicycle hanging on the wall in front of them.

"Because it's not." Garret released a heavy sigh and turned toward her. "Look, Darcy, the Station House didn't have any rooms. I had the night manager call the last motel near here and they were full, as well. So I brought you home with me."

Home? As in *his* home?

Garret tilted his head to the side and held both hands up, palms open. "I'm not a pervert or a rapist. And even though *you* could be an ax murderer, I'm going to take a chance and let you stay here for the night because I don't know what else to do."

He was exhausted. One glance into his weary gaze told her that. While she'd been dozing, he'd battled the elements to get them to safety and with no where else to take her—

"I'll sleep on the couch and you can have my bedroom. It has a lock on the door and I'll even give you a baseball bat if it makes you feel better, but honestly, you have nothing to worry about from me. Or Ethan."

That startled her. "Ethan?"

"My older brother lives here, too. I'll introduce you in the morning. He's completely safe. What do you say?"

What could she say? They were here and the thought of a bed compared to a booth in the hospital cafeteria was too tempting to resist. "Where's that bat?"

In response, Garret winked, then got out and grabbed their cases before leading the way into the house. Darcy followed him down a short hallway past a utility room, the kitchen and living room beyond.

"The bedroom is that way, first door on the right. Let me find some sheets and I'll change the bed for you."

"I'll do it." Her voice emerged scratchy so she cleared her throat and tried again. "I don't want you to go to any more trouble than you already have."

The melted snow left little diamond drops of water in his dark hair. They sparkled beneath the light.

"We'll change them together."

Garret left his briefcase near the couch and carried her suitcase into the bedroom. Within moments he located fresh sheets and they silently made up the bed together. The act was strangely intimate and brought a blush to her cheeks.

"Done. I'll get out of here so you can rest."

He grabbed some workout pants from a drawer and his toothbrush from the attached bath, then made one final trip into a walk-in closet where he retrieved a baseball bat. He held it out to her, and when she lifted a hand to accept it, he placed his free hand over hers.

"Sweet dreams, Darcy. To you and Butch both." He lowered his gaze to her stomach quickly before glancing back up and smiling at her, the look soft and sexy. Her heart raced and lost its rhythm. The feel of his touch, the expression on his face. The man was lethal. Letting go, Garret paused to lock the door on the way out.

She yawned as she donned her cold pajamas in the bathroom, brushed her teeth and climbed into bed, the bat propped within easy reach. The fresh scent of detergent and fabric softener smelled heavenly, but it was the other, more intriguing scent of Garret's cologne that had her pressing her nose into the pillow.

She slowly relaxed, amazed that the store-bought scent combined so well with the essential oils she'd rubbed on her neck earlier. Within moments she slipped into a cozy, dreamy state.

"So, Butch," she murmured, her hands on her belly, "what do you think? Is he for real?"

A firm, solid kick was her response—that and the sudden, urgent need to pee.

CHAPTER SEVEN

GARRET HAD JUST SET a skillet on the stove when he heard his bedroom door open. "In the kitchen!"

Darcy walked in bellyfirst, dressed in a brown velour track suit that matched her eyes and a blue T-shirt with a sparkly design on the front. Her curls were bouncy and shower fresh, her appearance alert although still more than a bit tired.

A rosy blush bloomed on her cheeks when she saw him. "Um…good morning." The color on her face deepened to a fiery pink. "I'm sorry I slept so late. You probably needed something from your room."

"I only just got moving myself. Did you sleep well?" He winced at the inane question. Anything was better than a hospital cafeteria.

"Yeah, I did. Thanks for lending me your room." Darcy stepped deeper into the kitchen. With a silent, sweeping glance she took in the black granite countertops, the sleek cabinets and stainless steel appliances. "This is nice."

"Thanks."

"I didn't see your brother. Is he still asleep?"

"Ethan's the surgeon on call this weekend. He left for work about five o'clock this morning because of an accident."

Darcy pursed her full lips at the news, the move making him want to lean over and brush his mouth across hers to ease the tension. Shock clenched his gut into a knot. Turning until he had his back to her, he planted his feet and swore softly. What was wrong with him? What was he doing? Thinking?

That her mouth would make any man want to kiss it?

"Did you burn yourself?"

"No." He waved the spatula. "Just forgot how to cook." Had the stress of his job pushed him off the deep end? Darcy was *pregnant*. Beyond the baby she carried and the complications that came with it, what about Joss? Harry? One wrong move would screw up everything.

"I hate to trouble you again, but I've got my stuff packed up. If you wouldn't mind giving me a ride to the garage to arrange things with Nick, I'll get out of your hair. I can take a cab to one of the motels from there."

Without uttering a word that might reveal his stupefying interest, Garret pointed the spatula toward the window. "Have you looked outside today?"

Darcy gasped. "It's *still* snowing?"

"Hasn't stopped all night. And—" he had to stop and inhale "—it's not supposed to clear up until tomorrow afternoon." Meaning they were snowbound for the next thirty-six hours—maybe more depending on the road conditions.

"You've *got* to be kidding me." She released a low, throaty groan. "I had no idea. I got up and saw how late it was and didn't even look out the window. I was hoping to get my car towed and find a room at one of the motels…"

Garret cracked an egg and muttered when there were more shells in the bowl than yolk. He set that one aside and grabbed another from the cabinet. "The whole town is shut down because of the storm. No one's going anywhere right now."

"But, Garret, I can't stay. We're strangers and I can't impose on you."

Strangers? Maybe, but it didn't seem that way. "I don't qualify as a friend?"

"Of course you do." Darcy's expression softened, her coffee-colored eyes filled with regret and wry amusement as she glanced over her shoulder at him, the light from the window turning her hair into an angel's halo. "But I wouldn't blame you if you wished you'd never stopped to help me."

This was a test. It had to be. He'd dragged his feet where Joss and commitment were concerned and now he was being tested. He faced a snowy weekend alone with a pretty woman who tempted him to think about her mouth.

He forced the direction of his thoughts into a U-turn. He wouldn't treat Darcy the way the baby's father obviously had. Nor would he subject Joss to the hurt that stemmed from betrayal. How had one simple act of kindness become so complicated?

Things are only as complicated as you let them get.

He watched Darcy nibble her lower lip. She was a worrier. The baby, the wreck, the snow and getting to wherever it was in Indiana she was going. The best thing for him to do was make things here as *un*-complicated as possible for them both.

Drawn even though he warned himself to keep his distance, he moved to stand behind her and stare out at the snow. "I couldn't have lived with myself if I'd left you sitting by the side of the road last night, Darcy. Just like I couldn't have left you sitting in the cafeteria. I'd do it again without question. Stop worrying." He managed a strained chuckle and backed away when the smell of her made him want to step closer. "Admit it, you slept a lot better in my bed."

The image of which was now firmly ensconced in his head. He scraped a hand over his face, picturing her warm and drowsy, the two of them spooning.

"You know I did."

He had to clear his throat to speak. "So, we'll make the best of the situation until the roads clear up." And he'd keep his distance, ignore the scent of her that drew him like a bee to a flower and—

See if I pass the test.

JOCELYN PIERSON SHIVERED as she pulled her keys from her pocket to let herself into the back door of her dream-come-true. Her art gallery was the bane of her father's existence. It was scheduled to open in a couple months—albeit later than she'd hoped, thanks to a series of delays—and she was extraordinarily proud of her achievement. Not bad for someone with "a soft little brain and poor judgment" according to her father.

The wind whipped up the moment she pulled her keys from the lock, and the force of it rocked her already-unsteady stance. She fell against the door with a muffled gasp, the keys tumbling through the metal-grate stairs into the snow below.

Muttering words guaranteed to get any good Southern girl's mouth washed out with soap, she turned to retrace her steps and found herself staring down at Garret's best friend.

"Go on inside, I'll get them." Tobias Richardson jerked his head toward the building to confirm his words, his nose and cheeks red from exposure.

She grabbed the handle to open the utility door and then had to fight the wind to close it behind her. Her hair stuck to her lipstick, her eyes watered after being out so long and her toes had gone numb twenty minutes ago while getting breakfast. She'd packed a bag but hadn't thought to bring snacks to eat. Luckily the diner was open. She tossed her bagged brunch aside, wishing she'd brought something warmer and more comfortable to wear.

Joss hurried to repair the damage and make herself presentable, but the hair clip caught in the tangles created by the wind. Just when she'd gathered the mass into some semblance of order, the door behind her opened. The wind blew snow through the back room, strewing papers, scattering the dirt she'd swept into a pile but hadn't disposed of. The blast of cold air ripped her hair from her hands, and all attempts at fixing her appearance vanished.

Tobias pushed the door shut and stomped his feet on the rug.

Desperate, Jocelyn smoothed her hair as best she could and tried to pretend it wasn't a disaster. "Thanks for getting my keys."

He moved toward her with a slight smile on his big, dopey face, her keys dangling from his hand. She'd always considered Tobias handsome in an awkward, gauche sort of way. He had a tall, lean body with the rolling gait of a western wrangler and sun-streaked, mud-brown hair that was forever in need of a trim. By far his eyes were his best, and worst, feature. They were a startling golden brown so light they looked yellow. Hawk's eyes, Garret had once said. The term fit.

"Here." He held out the keys and she looked down. His hands were chapped, the calluses on the sides of his fingers white with age.

"Thank you. How's Maria? I heard they were going to induce her on Wednesday if she didn't go into labor this weekend."

"She had the baby at one o'clock this morning. A girl, just like expected." Tobias released the keys. Their fingers brushed during the exchange and, as if the act had tainted him with some incurable disease, he rubbed his hand discreetly against his leg, then lifted it and pushed his hair back from his face.

She turned, absurdly hurt by his behavior. With a silent, appraising glance he criticized her clothes, her appearance, everything, making her well aware that he thought her less than worthy of Garret. Once more she tried to gather her hair without making too much fuss.

"Leave it down. It doesn't look as stiff."

Stiff? She hesitated for a split second, then continued with her task. "Daddy always says professional women do not have wild hair, nor do debutantes."

"And you are that."

She turned, her gaze narrowing on him. "Pardon me?"

"A professional woman." Tobias lifted one of his

ugly hands to indicate their surroundings. "The place seems to be coming together."

It was a mess. She knew it. He knew it. Why pretend? Normally he wouldn't. She'd often wondered what she'd done to earn his hostility, but figured her relationship with Garret topped Tobias's list of her many negative attributes. Then there was his mother and her role as the Piersons' maid once upon a time. Tobias hadn't liked Jocelyn then, either, referring to her as "princess" in his mocking tone. "I'm running a little behind schedule, but I'll catch up. I stayed here last night and got quite—"

"What?"

The vehemence in his tone surprised her. "I beg your pardon?"

"You stayed here? By yourself? Did Garret stay with you?"

Joss couldn't believe his nerve. She shifted her weight onto one hip and crossed her arms over her less-than-stellar chest. "No, he didn't. But somehow I managed to survive all by myself."

He looked as though he'd swallowed a lemon. "I meant with the weather as bad as it is and with this place in such a state—"

"You just said it was coming together."

"I lied. It looks like hell, but I didn't want to hurt your feelings."

"Like you care about that. You just informed me my hair looks *stiff*."

"What do you expect when it's always scraped back and stuck to your head?"

Jocelyn stared at him, her mouth open in shock. Of all the—

"You shouldn't have stayed here by yourself. That's all I'm saying. It's dangerous."

"And you think it's dangerous because…what? I'm such a ditz I can't lock a door or turn on the alarm system? Can't call the police if someone were to break in? Can't use one of the many metal rods lying about to whack someone over the head if I needed to?"

He shuffled his feet as though he was suddenly being attacked by ants—or metal rods. "I forgot you had an alarm."

"I know how to work it, too," she said in her sweetest, most saccharine Southern-belle voice. "But I guess that shows your opinion of me, doesn't it? Just say it, Tobias. You think I'm dumb. I'm so dumb, in fact, that Garret shouldn't be with me. And that 'professional woman' comment? We both know what you meant—it was a shot because I *was* a debutante. But, for the record, some of the most enterprising, take-charge women in this part of the country were *debutantes*."

"I don't want to argue with you, dammit, I—"

"Then don't. Just tell me why you're here and get o—" She broke off, but it was too late. They both knew what she'd been about to say. "I—I'm sorry. That was very rude."

He pulled an envelope from his pocket and shoved it at her, his unusual eyes glittering with anger and what looked to be...hurt?

"Tobias—"

"Make sure you lock up and set the alarm."

He was out the door in seconds. As though taking his side, the wind tore at her hair yet again before Tobias yanked the panel shut with a loud bang.

She opened the envelope and choked at the embossed slip inside. Coughing, wheezing, she collapsed against a crate, digging the paper from within to confirm the truth she already knew. It wasn't... surely it *wasn't*.

But it was. Oh, shoot, what had she done?

She was now going to have to apologize to one of the most obnoxious men on the planet.

CHAPTER EIGHT

"TOBIAS, WAIT!" Jocelyn hurried out the door after him. "Wait!" she called again, catching him halfway down the stairs. He didn't stop. "Tobias, please."

Manners did the trick. He turned to stare up at her, his thick eyebrows low over his eyes. "What do you want?"

The temperature made her teeth chatter. "C-can you come back inside for a minute?" Remembering what had made him stop, she added, "Please?"

Tobias ran his hand over his hair and messed it even more. Didn't he ever get his hair cut? She bit her tongue to keep from saying something else she shouldn't and waited for him to make up his mind. Stubborn man.

It bothered her that he didn't like her. It didn't matter, of course. But he was Garret's best friend and she had enough good girl in her to want everyone to like her. Including him. But the fact that Tobias behaved as though he couldn't stand to be in her presence—that he didn't approve of Garret's love for her—irritated her to no end.

Was he going to make her stand out here all day in the cold? Finally he released a disgruntled sigh and retraced his steps, following her into the gallery's back room.

"Thank you for the permit." It came out badly, as though her gratitude wasn't sincere or she didn't appreciate the effort he'd made to get the permit. "It was very nice of you to do that."

"You're welcome."

That's it? No explanation as to *why* he'd done it? *Champagne and beer don't mix, Jocelyn Renee. But you won't ever forget it again, will you?* Her father's overbearing voice rang in her head.

No, she wouldn't forget. But in that moment she felt as though she owed Tobias a warning about her father. Over the past couple of years, Daddy had gotten in more than his fair share of snide comments about the son of their former maid, making it clear he wanted no one in his family associating with Tobias. Even though Daddy hadn't yet set down the law with Garret—as he was wont to do with her—she knew he didn't approve of the friendship between Garret and Tobias. It was only a matter of time before her father started vocalizing his displeasure and pressuring Garret to cease all contact with Tobias. And her father would not be subtle or fair. He wouldn't hesitate to use her to control Garret.

Regardless of her feelings about the man, Tobias deserved to know what her father would try to do.

Tobias shifted his too-big feet. She needed to say something, tell him that Garret was stronger, that he was a good friend, a good man. That Daddy would never control Garret the way he did her. But the words wouldn't come. Truth was Garret and her father were very close. They had been for years, even longer than she and Garret had dated.

Looking extremely put out by her continued silence, Tobias sighed. "Was that all you wanted?"

"No." She cleared her throat and lifted her chin, determined to make peace if it killed her. "I wanted to know why you did it."

His shoulders lifted and lowered in a tense shrug. "Don't get too ahead of yourself, princess. I was at the courthouse and saw your name on a pending file. It was no big deal."

Oh, how she despised that nickname. Her father had called her that, too. A pretty princess in a tower who should be seen and not heard. "I don't get it."

"What is there to get?" he asked impatiently.

She made herself meet his unusual eyes. "I don't get *why*. You don't like me. Don't pretend you do because we both know better. Why would you go out of your way to get this for me? Seems to me you'd like to see me fail."

Indecently thick lashes lowered over his gaze. "That's not true. But you need the permit to open, and I thought I'd save Garret the hassle of having to get it for you."

So he didn't approve of her gallery, either? "I would've handled the permit myself. I've managed to get all the others. I admit this one has been a problem but— I appreciate the help. I asked Garret to see if he could hurry the process but he's been so busy he hasn't had the chance. I was going to remind him again when things settled down."

"You would've run out of time waiting for that to happen. Your father's got Garret's nose to the grindstone."

She knew well what that felt like. She'd been raised beneath her father's overwhelming aggression and constant disapproval. Never measuring up. Never doing enough or else doing it *wrong*. Right now he blamed her for Garret not proposing yet, but what woman wanted to nag a man into marrying her?

"I'd better go."

Tobias looked bored by the stilted conversation. And there he went, tugging on his hair again like a big old dog scratching at his ear. But she had to do something. She couldn't imagine spending her married life to Garret, having his best friend glare at her all the time. The tension between them had to end. "Tobias—"

"Toby."

"You look more like a Tobias." Why had she said that? She swallowed audibly. "Anyway, please wait. I owe you another apology."

"For what?"

It wasn't easy to bring up a subject that happened so long ago. "I'm sorry I didn't speak up. Years ago. That day at the house. Those girls were awful."

"You mean your friends?"

She faltered again. "They weren't my friends. Not really. Not at all, if you want the truth." He didn't look surprised by the confession. "I should've said something to them when they began saying those things. It probably embarrassed you—"

"It was a long time ago." A ruddy hue crawled up his neck to his cheeks.

She stared, dumbstruck. Was that it? She'd felt badly about it, but he'd acted like a jerk and— He was *embarrassed?* Nervous around her because that happened years ago? Was that why he kept fidgeting? And the way he barked at her and glared and acted so brooding when the three of them were together? Was that him trying to cope with the rudeness of a teenage girl who'd become his best friend's date?

How could she not have realized? "I should've

said something. I didn't speak up and that was… unkind. And then my father didn't pay you after all the hard work— I wish you had kept the check I sent you."

"It wasn't your bill to pay. I didn't want your money."

She realized now she'd only made the situation worse by doing that. How could she have been so blind? "But you earned it." And she wouldn't have missed the money. She knew he'd needed it, though, to help support his mother and little sister. "How is your mother?"

Tobias rubbed a knuckle against his mouth. "She's fine. She likes being a grandma again."

"Good. That's good." She saw a clipboard lying nearby and picked it up to have something to do with her hands. "I'm glad things are going so well for you. All of you. Anyway, thank you. Again. You've done Garret and me a huge favor."

His mouth pulled up in one of his smirking grins, one that lit his face and made his eyes crinkle at the corners, giving him a devilish quality. The expression emphasized the deep cleft in his chin. She hadn't found those sexy since her crush on Tom Selleck, but on Tobias… Well, he had a certain quality. She'd have to give him more thought. Think of a female friend he might appeal to. Someone nice and down-to-earth. Heaven knew she owed him that.

Tobias turned away but paused. "Did you have to clean the pool?"

The question caught her by surprise, although it shouldn't have. She laughed, remembering her father's rage and her secret delight that someone had gotten even with him and his tyranny. "No. He called a service to do that. But they charged him three times what he owed you."

A gruff chuckle erupted from his chest. "Served him right."

"I agree." He looked startled by her agreement and faced her with an expression she couldn't quite decipher. The metal clip dug into her hand.

Tobias glanced around at the assortment of crates she needed to unpack, canvases she'd prepared for hanging, none of which could be done until the walls were painted. "You're going to try to do all this yourself?"

"I, uh, hired someone who was supposed to have come today to help me. With the weather, we thought it best to cancel."

"Would you like me to help?"

Was he serious? Or just being polite and making a peace offering after their talk? Probably the second, but did it matter? They seemed to have crossed a bridge in their relationship. Maybe he'd stop all the glaring and come to terms with her marrying his best friend.

"That would be great. You don't have plans for the day?"

For the first time since she remembered meeting him, Tobias's eyes warmed when he looked at her and shrugged. "Where do we start?"

WHILE GARRET SECLUDED himself in his home office to work and to call Nick about her car, Darcy took care of the breakfast dishes and picked up around the surprisingly clean bachelor pad. The two guys were neater than she ever hoped to be.

Shaking her head, she looked up, her gaze caught by the weather outside. Everything was buried beneath a ruler's worth of snow and ice. All she'd needed was one more day of driving and she could've made it to her destination. At least close. *Close only counts in horseshoes and hand grenades.*

She rolled her eyes at the juvenile saying. The thick layer of snow made her wonder about her car. What if it was so covered that Nick couldn't find it? Or worse, that some other driver hadn't seen it and slid into it after hitting that same patch of ice she had? What shape was her poor car in? How much money would she need to repair it? Growing up dependent upon an ever-changing stream of "uncles" for food and rent had made her the stand-on-her-own-two-feet type, but the repairs and hospital stay could easily wipe out the majority of her nest egg. Living in Miami wasn't cheap—yet another reason to go home to Indiana where a dollar stretched a little further.

Garret's footfalls sounded on the hardwood floor outside the kitchen and she turned to see him looking as disgruntled as she felt. "Uh-oh, something wrong?"

His gaze swept over the stove and lingered on the now-spotless sink. "Yeah, but we'll get to that in a minute. I got hold of Nick. He won't be able to tow your car until the state of emergency is lifted, but he did say he'd make you a priority."

Being made a priority was great, but the weight on her shoulders pressed heavier than ever. She hated feeling so helpless, so dependent.

Garret ran a hand over his short hair. "Look, Darcy, I didn't bother calling the motels about vacancies. Right now, even if someone did check out and attempt to leave town, I wouldn't want to take you out on the roads. It's too dangerous, and you can't risk another scare after what you went through last night."

She felt like such a pain, but since it was the smart thing to do, she forced herself to nod. Waiting out the storm here might be best, but it didn't make her conscience rest any easier.

"Are you okay with spending another night here?"

"If you don't mind, I suppose that's fine." She hated

imposing on Garret this way, hated feeling as if her life was racing out of control and she couldn't stop the skid. At the same time, she was grateful for Garret's gentlemanly behavior and the fact that she wasn't stuck in some grimy hotel room she couldn't afford. "I can't tell you how much I appreciate your help, Garret. I keep saying it, but it's true. I don't know what I would have done without you. And I'm happy to pitch in while I'm here. It's the least I can do."

He gave her a smiling yet disapproving look and heat bloomed in her face. Scruffy had never looked so sexy on a guy.

"Yeah, about that. You're supposed to be resting, not cleaning up the dishes." Garret tilted his head to one side and crossed his arms over his chest. The move delineated the muscles beneath his long-sleeved T-shirt. "Didn't I tell you to leave those?"

"You cooked. It was only fair."

Garret had been gorgeous in his dark suit and overcoat last night, but this morning he looked even more so in worn running pants and a lightweight U of T shirt that had seen better days. Both molded his body, and his size gave her butterflies. *No, definitely not a hardship.*

"Quit worrying about imposing. You just follow the doctor's orders about getting some rest. Take it easy, and pretend you're in a messy hotel."

He said that with a handsome grin, one that emphasized the deep creases bracketing his mouth. He worked hard, but he laughed hard, too. She liked that. And the way his hair stuck up at odd angles. Too cute. Just because she was pregnant didn't mean she was blind.

"This place is a far cry from messy. It's hard to believe two bachelors live here."

"Yeah, well, you can thank Ethan for that. He has a neat streak a mile wide. Just make yourself at home. When the snow lets up, we'll get you where you want to be."

Such a gentleman. "Thank you."

"You're welcome. Now I'm going to go grab a shower. While I do that, why don't you go call your mother?" Garret walked to the counter and jotted something down on a notepad beside the phone. "Maybe you'll feel better if you hear her voice. Here's the number to give her."

It was a sweet thing to say. And for a guy who obviously loved his family and was obviously loved by them, she supposed that would be the case, but her mom? They really weren't that close. Although, to be fair, she did say she'd help watch the baby. Darcy accepted the slip of paper and smiled. "Thanks."

As she watched him leave the kitchen Garret seemed like true hero material. The manners, the consideration. His unbelievable good looks—a regular

Raoul Bova look-alike. What more could a girl ask? If all Garret's brothers resembled him… *Da—*

Shaking her head, she remembered her vow to clean up her language. She so did not want her baby sounding like a guest on *Jerry Springer.* Her life had had more than its share of swear-perfect moments, but it was time to change; otherwise, her baby's first word would be of the four-letter variety.

Darcy left the kitchen and made her way to Garret's bedroom to the phone, smiling at the sound of Garret whistling farther down the hall. Door shut, her footsteps dragged as she made her way over to the bed. *Come on, Mom, be home. Be there for me.*

Seconds later she waited and counted the rings. Two. Three. Four. *Pick up!* A click sounded, then her mother's recorded message played. Where *was* she? Surely her mother wasn't off with another new guy? Darcy supported the idea of her mom finding true love and living happily ever after. But that was unlikely to happen with the losers her mother seemed to gravitate to.

The beep sounded. "Hi, Mom, it's me. Are you there? Pick up, it's important." She twisted the phone cord around her finger. "I'm still in Tennessee. My car has to be towed and repaired, and— The hospital released me last night, but I'm stuck in the snowstorm."

Out of nowhere, hope soared. Was her mom on

her way here to check on her? Had her mom finally put Darcy ahead of her latest guy? *Please, just once let me come first.* "Call me as soon as you get my messages, okay? *Call me.*" She left the number and murmured goodbye, hating the tears that thickened her voice toward the end.

She couldn't help it though. Everyone deserved at least one grand gesture in their life. Deserved to have someone, a loved one, do something big, something *meaningful,* that showed them how much they were loved. Something that declared loud and clear, "Screw the world, you're more important!"

Lying back on the bed, she squirmed until she was comfortable, and sighed, tired even though she woke up only a little while ago. "I'll do anything for you, Jordan. I'll give you so many grand gestures you won't ever doubt you're loved," she whispered, rubbing her stomach. "I just want someone to do the same for me."

CHAPTER NINE

TOBY WIPED the sweat from his forehead and stared at Jocelyn. He had no business being here. People would talk if they found out, speculate about what happened between him and his best friend's almost-fiancée during these hours alone.

"Something wrong?"

Pulled from his thoughts, he searched her upturned face for any sign of the teenage bitch she'd been. Surprisingly, he didn't see a trace of the girl who'd received a red BMW for her sweet sixteen. "Is it straight?"

Jocelyn took a few steps back and eyed the section of gallery wall they'd been working on. "Tilt it to the right just a smidge."

Who knew it took this much effort to decorate a *wall?* They'd finished painting the one wall, assembled some shelving units, then started the tedious process of unpacking, displaying and hanging—and rehanging—the art. Sighing, he did as ordered.

"Wait. Back the other way. Perfect!" She gave

him a million-dollar smile, and he thought back to middle school when her mouth had been full of braces. He'd had them at the time, too, and more than once he'd dreamed of locking metal with her.

She tucked her hair behind her shell-shaped ear, drawing his attention to the one-carat diamond studs in her lobes. Garret hadn't blinked at the price of those. Over the past couple of years his buddy had dragged Toby into many jewelry stores to help pick something out for Jocelyn. Fact was, Toby had been the one to choose these earrings for her. They'd reminded him of her when he'd spied them—elegant and tasteful. Classy.

The same was true with the engagement ring Garret had purchased but had yet to give her. Garret had bought the damn thing, but *Toby* had been the one who'd selected it after shaking his head at the ugly monstrosity Garret had favored. Didn't Garret know Jocelyn's tastes at all?

"Are you going to stay up there all day?"

He didn't move. "Depends. You got anything else you want done?"

Her cheeks blushed prettily when she looked at her watch and gasped. "Oh, it's late! Where did the time go?" She gaped up at him. "Tobias, I'm so sorry. I had no idea the day had flown by. I was just so happy to be getting things done."

He'd noticed. That was why he'd stayed. Because

she'd given him so many smiles and glances from beneath her long lashes. Because doing these tasks had made her happy and he'd liked seeing her happy. Maybe a little too much. "I'm glad to have helped."

"Well, I'm sorry to have kept you so long. With this storm it's going to take you forever and a day to get home." She smoothed a hand over her hair, drawing attention to the clasp she'd stuck back in.

He'd wanted to remove the thing all day, make her look the way she had that morning. She'd been more approachable then, whereas now she looked almost uncomfortable in her own skin. A little girl playing dress-up; her hair fixed—if messier than normal—lipstick in place. A smudge on the pantsuit she'd worn to muck around the gallery. Who worked in pantsuits, and designer ones at that?

"Is something wrong? You're frowning."

Caught unaware, he shook his head. "Don't you own any sweats?"

"Why do you ask?"

It was none of his business what she wore—or who she dated. "Never mind." He moved down the ladder and shoved aside the thoughts of Garret and Jocelyn together. He had no right to think of her that way.

"Sweats would be more comfortable, but Daddy hates them. Says women should look like women, not sports jocks."

"You'd still look like a woman, trust me." He said

the words deliberately, knew it would send her into a tizzy of ums and ohs and fussing hands. She smoothed her fingers over her hair to capture all the baby-fine strands that had escaped, tugged at her jacket and pulled it down over her small breasts and raised her eyebrows high, her smooth forehead wrinkling.

"He says it's one of the rules of business, to always be presentable. I never know who might walk through the door whether here or at home. He insists Mother and I look our best at all times. Guess old habits don't die."

"You're presentable." Toby stepped off the ladder and walked to where she stood. "Your father's rules aren't the be-all and end-all, Jocelyn." He lifted his hand and tortured himself by grasping a flyaway tendril between his thumb and forefinger and tucking it behind her ear. "Beauty is in the eye of the beholder. Some men don't mind a woman looking a little ruffled."

"Garret—"

She stopped whatever it was she'd been about to say.

But the spell was broken. At the mention of his best friend, he berated himself for playing with fire. The diamond studs winked at him beneath the gallery lights, the reminder that she was out of his league transmitted loud and clear.

"I'd better go." He meant to step away. But the

allure of Jocelyn—all striking blue eyes and full lips that he'd bet his hard-earned money had no collagen assistance—held him in place. Sophistication rolled off her from her pointy, spiky-heeled boots to her sculpted nose—another present from Daddy because, heaven forbid, her nose hadn't been perfect the way it was.

He'd like to see her in sweats. And drunk, just once. She'd be a silly drunk.

"You're staring again. Are you sure nothing is wrong?"

Something was wrong, all right. Having these powerful feelings for Jocelyn—for his best friend's almost-fiancée—was more than wrong. He'd best get used to wanting but never getting because the situation wasn't going to change. Jocelyn would never leave Garret, and eventually Garret would marry her. "Positive." Toby glanced at his watch. "I need to get out of here. And you should think about doing the same."

"Of course. Thank you again."

Needing air, Toby headed for the door. If he were a gentleman he'd wait for her. He'd lock up and clean the snow from her car. He'd drive behind her to ensure she arrived home safely. But he wasn't a gentleman. He was a man grasping for a shred of decency so he didn't give in to the urge to do all kinds of wicked and sinful things with this woman.

"Tobias, wait."

Hand on the door, he gritted his teeth and paused.

"I meant what I said earlier. About everything that happened years ago," she said in a rush. "I'd like us to be friends. For Garret's sake if nothing else."

He couldn't stop the smirk forming on his lips. *For Garret's sake.* "Okay. Sure, why not."

"Really?"

Toby pulled the door open, resigned. "Yeah."

THAT EVENING Darcy lifted her finger to her nape and smoothed lavender oil on her pulse point, inhaling deeply and appreciating how the scent instantly soothed her.

"Are you feeling okay?"

Garret's voice startled her. After a day spent alternately working, helping her with the meals, he'd disappeared into his thoughts. He'd been sitting here looking at the movie playing on the plasma screen yet he didn't appear to be actually watching it. Something was obviously on his mind, but the remote expression on his face kept her from asking. "I'm fine. What about you?"

He flashed her a fake I'm-okay, you're-okay smile. "Sorry, I've been distracted."

"Headache?"

"Yeah. I get them sometimes."

"Want to talk about whatever's stressing you?"

Darcy twisted the lid on the tiny bottle of expensive oil before returning it to the case and pulling out another. She repeated the process, tipping the bottle until a drop of oil sparkled on her finger, rubbing it on her neck and inhaling the fragrance.

"There's a lot on my plate right now."

She looked at him, taking in the little lines of strain around his eyes and mouth. Poor guy really was hurting. He needed a good massage or a long vacation. Better yet, both. "Do you work every weekend? Ever take any time off?"

A shudder blanked his features, as if he'd heard the question countless times before. "Things are more hectic than usual. The hospital was recently purchased by a bigger one and there is a lot of red tape to get through." He nodded toward her hands. "What is that stuff? I thought you smelled different. Is that why?"

She pretended outrage. "Are you saying I *smell?*" Her ploy worked because his expression turned teasing.

"That last one smelled like Christmas so it's a good smell."

Darcy held the latest bottle out for his perusal. "It's an essential oil. I use them in my massage therapy sessions."

Garret leaned forward a little and sniffed. "Cypress?"

"Very good."

"I can't take credit. My mother and grandmother really get into decorating the house at Christmas. They always have fresh greenery and cinnamon, stuff like that."

"Sounds nice."

"It is. What about you? What was your house like?"

"Oh, nothing spectacular. My mom was so afraid of setting the house on fire that we had a fake tree. One of the small ones that could be scrunched up and put into storage."

"Not us. Real trees, all the way."

"Trees? More than one?"

Garret got up and moved to sit beside her. He plucked the case of oils from her lap, held it up to his nose and sniffed cautiously.

"Yeah. Sometimes one in every room, sometimes more. They always had a theme, so needless to say my mother's ornament collection is massive. Now it fills the attic."

"I'll bet they're beautiful."

More than anything else, for some reason the number and type of Christmas trees articulated their vastly different upbringings. What would growing up in that house have been like?

"What's this?"

"Huh?" Her gaze was drawn to his lips when he smiled.

"Where did you go?"

Heat crept into her face. "Baby fog," she said by way of an excuse. "My mind slips into la-la land a lot. What did you say?"

"What's this one?"

The bottle looked fragile in his big hand. "That's a blend of several of the oils. It helps with anxiety and depression."

"Wasn't this the one you used?"

She couldn't hold his gaze. "I'm pregnant, the father is a no-good, lying bas—*louse. And* I'm stuck in a snowstorm because I wrecked the first new car I was ever able to buy. Depressed? Maybe just a little."

"Things will get better, Darcy. Nick will have your car fixed up good as new."

"Maybe."

"Not *maybe*. You'll be good to go in no time."

Yeah, but would she still have a place to go *to?*

"Come on, talk to me. What are you thinking about?"

She didn't want to unload her burdens on him, didn't want him to know all the nasty details of her life she was embarrassed about and couldn't change.

"If you tell me to butt out, I will. But I'm not going to stop asking until you do."

She liked persistence. And the timbre of his voice sent a shiver down her spine. But how silly was that? Seven and a half months pregnant and she felt shivers?

Darcy inhaled, sighed. Maybe talking would help. It would distract her from her fascination with her host if nothing else. "My mom had me when she was seventeen. I never knew my dad. He and my mom broke up before I was born. Life was hard for her. And despite always, *always* saying I'd never wind up like my mother, here I am. I've followed in her footsteps by having a baby alone." She tried to smile, but couldn't. "I mean, sure, I'm older than she was and I have career skills. But sometimes I'm not sure I'm ready to be a mother. Would the baby be better off with someone else? You know…adopted. But then I feel it move and I know I wouldn't be able to live with myself if I gave it up."

Garret's hand touched her shoulder. "Do you have to do this alone? It takes two to make a baby."

"Stephen wants nothing to do with it. Us."

"That's his loss, Darcy. As to being a mom, I'd say every woman has doubts. Wonders if she's doing a good job."

"The books say it's normal but…"

"But?"

"But I've always wanted too much. Wanted way too much."

"How so?"

She stared at the big screen and saw her plans for her life disintegrating. "When I had a baby I wanted to be married to the man I'd spend the rest of my life with, someone who'd share the good and the bad. And now, with everything that's gone on, I just don't know how that can happen." She paused. "I see these elderly couples holding hands and talking, and I wonder what have they done—what secrets do they know—to make it so many years together. I don't know anything about that kind of staying power, so how could I have it?"

Garret took the bottle from her hand and put it in the case, then snagged her fingers and squeezed them gently. The trace of oils warmed with the contact of their skin, releasing the scent. "You can have anything you set your mind to. And I don't doubt you'll give your baby the best life you possibly can."

"I will." *I promise.*

"You're better off without that guy. Instead of wondering why Dad doesn't love him or her, your baby will grow up knowing your love and protection. You're saving your baby from that kind of insecurity."

"I don't ever want the baby to feel like she's a burden or a mistake. Stephen was a mistake, but not this baby."

"You are going to be a great mom." Garret handed the case to her. "Now tell me about the rest of those. What do they do?"

She welcomed Garret's attempt to distract her. To get her mind off whatever the future might hold. But she could see what the effort was costing him by the pain in his eyes, by the way he turned his head, rubbed his temple.

"Listen, forget the oils." She hesitated, then jumped up from the couch as fast as her beached-whale body could travel. "It's obvious your head is killing you and you're sitting there trying to take care of me when I'm the one who should be helping you. Have you ever had a massage?"

CHAPTER TEN

GARRET STARED at her, concern changing to confusion and then pure leeriness. No doubt he was thinking she'd gone off a hormonal cliff. From sad and reflective to happy and talking massages in less than five minutes? She supposed it would freak a few people out, but the sight of him in pain bothered her.

"No, I haven't, but it's okay. You don't—"

"I *do*. You want me to be comfortable here, right?"

"Right, but—"

"I can help you. I'm feeling really bad about you getting stuck with me and then—" she waved a hand toward where she'd been sitting "—going all gushy like I did. No guy wants a woman dumping on them, especially not when you look like your head is about to explode."

He chuckled and rubbed his neck. "I asked you to dump on me. I could tell something was bothering you and you needed to talk. Better out than in where it upsets Penelope."

She made a face at his attempt at a name.

Penelope? Unless Cruz was attached to the end of it or there was a lot of cash in the bank account, the kid wouldn't stand a chance on the playground. It was yet another example of how different their lives were. "I'm not doing anything here but eating your food and kicking you out of your bed."

"You haven't been a problem, Darcy. If I thought you were I would've braved the roads today. Ever think of that? But I didn't because I've enjoyed our time together. Maybe too much."

Too much? She smiled. "Me, too."

"Good. So don't worry about me sleeping out here. I don't sleep that well, anyway."

"I know."

He looked at her, confusion apparent. "How do you know?"

"I can tell." She shrugged. "This is what I do, remember? No offense, but you're as tense as a crossbow. Your head hurts, you keep twisting and turning your head and neck, shrugging your shoulders, and you've been blinking a lot, like people do when they're running on fumes. But I can fix all that *and* I can practically guarantee that you'll sleep tonight. Come on, aren't you just the tiniest bit interested? I'm not offering to do anything kinky or weird."

"I wasn't thinking that."

Heat flooded into her face. She'd been joking, but

once the words were said she would have sworn he was thinking something along those lines.

And for one rash, split second she was thinking it, too. Obviously, her hormones were on an upswing. Sex at this stage of her pregnancy? With a man she'd just met? *So* not going to happen. "Right, I—I wanted to be clear. I charge a hundred dollars or more for my services and I don't want you to get the wrong idea and think something else is happening. Not that you would."

"A hundred bucks?"

"Yeah." Oh, he was definitely curious now. "What do you say?"

"Darcy, this isn't necessary. You don't need to repay me."

"Look, I know a massage doesn't come close to making up for all that you've done, but it would help you and that would make me feel better."

"Why is this so important to you?"

She could lie and say it wasn't, but something about the look on his face compelled her to be honest. "Because I've been on my own since I was seventeen and I haven't taken charity from anyone. I don't want to start now."

"Seventeen? Is that why you identified with Nick?"

Darcy shrugged. She was more than a little ashamed of her upbringing, which Stephen's parents had combed through, then used to make their points for why she shouldn't be with him. After hearing Garret talk about his family, she didn't want him doing the same. "You may not see my staying here as a handout, but I do." She placed her hands over her belly. "I don't want Spike to think it's okay to mooch off people. You'd help me save face with my baby if you agree."

Garret regarded her a long moment, a sexy half smile pulling at his lips. "Well, we can't have *Spike* thinking that about his mother. What would I have to do?"

Darcy nibbled her lip, suddenly not sure her hormone-heavy body could handle him stripping down to his skivvies like her other clients. This was her job. One she did well with the utmost professionalism. But Garret was *not* her ordinary client.

"Nothing drastic. We're not set up here for a full massage, but I think your back and shoulders are the biggest problem so, um, just take off your shirt." She wouldn't ask for more. It was too intimate, too personal a thing, given the setting. Had they been in a more clinical environment she would be able to view him objectively as a series of body systems in various stages of distress. But with Garret on the couch, in his home…

He stood before she had time to do more than take in a steadying breath. He unbuttoned the shirt and for some reason the sight left her a little dizzy and thigh-clenchingly aware of him. Yes, she'd noticed how handsome he was, but a lot of guys were handsome. Stephen had been gorgeous with his Latin heritage. She'd worked on models. Even an actor or two. But with every button Garret released, she saw more of his chest and—*whew!*

A light dusting of black hair covered Garret's upper chest and pecs before tapering into the waistband of his pants. He didn't have a blatant six-pack, but his stomach was tight and firm, defined. He was beautiful. All big boned and raw sensuality.

She never got nervous when she worked on a client, but Garret was different. After everything that had happened between her and Stephen, she honestly thought it would be a long, long time before she noticed a man again. In any way. Before her pregnancy had started to show, she'd had invitations from guys saying they'd make her forget all about Stephen. She hadn't been the slightest bit tempted, but right now…

Before she could entertain more thoughts about exploring all that exposed skin in a purely unprofessional way, she turned to arrange her oils on the coffee table. That done, she grabbed the sheet Garret had slept on the night before and spread it over the expensive leather, busying herself so she wouldn't have to look at him. "Lie down when you're ready."

She found some gentle-sounding music on the television and waited until she heard Garret lower himself onto the couch. She peeked at the broad expanse of his back, the strength and texture of his skin. So much temptation. But there was no changing her mind now.

The first step was getting him used to her touch. Darcy grabbed the odorless massage oil, warmed it in her hands, then placed her palms on his shoulders and spread the oil on his skin. Careful to keep the pressure light, she smoothed it down his back, then started at the base of his spine and with increasing force, ran her thumbs up both sides. Just as she'd suspected. Tighter than a drum.

Starting at the dimpled base of his spine—so cute!—again, she stroked harder and felt Garret stiffen, as if he struggled to suppress a groan. Smiling, she repeated the motion, feeling him tense up whenever she got to the worst spot between his shoulders. Finally he gave in. A rough growl of pleasure emerged, one that had her holding her breath and suppressing yet another shiver.

"Darcy, that feels…good."

"See?" Ordinarily, she kept her voice pitched low so as soothe and not startle her client. Doing so now didn't require much effort given the surprising huskiness of her tone.

Moving outward, she found the trigger points in his shoulders and worked out the knotted muscles there. The poor guy was a mess.

Garret sighed and angled his head away from her, his eyes drifting closed. She could still see his profile, however, and after a few minutes, the tiny lines on his face eased. Guitar music played in the background, the strumming slow and soft. Beautiful songs that blended together with barely a break in rhythm.

Now that he was relaxed, she could introduce the scented oils. She left one hand on his back to maintain contact and grabbed one of the bottles she'd arranged on the table. Roman chamomile filled the air.

Darcy brushed her fingertips up his back in light strokes to spread the oil, then firmed her touch at the base and started up again. Reaching his neck, her palms slid over his shoulders and squeezed. Another sexy-rough sigh escaped him. The sound echoed through her and she tuned into the feel of his silky, black hair as it curled over her thumbs, the steely strength of the corded muscles beneath his skin. She shook her head slightly to snap her out of the sensual spell. This was a *massage,* not a seduction.

With renewed purpose, she moved her hands in long, rhythmic patterns, gently pulling and loosening the muscles, working out the knots with single-minded determination that she would help him sleep.

One by one she added more oils and the scents of spruce and blue tansy filled the air. The knots behind his shoulder blades slowly released, as did those in his neck, too. The longer she massaged, the more pliant Garret became, and she loved the husky sounds he made as he lost himself in the experience.

Certain clients had a hard time relinquishing control because of body image or some other insecurity, but Garret was doing wonderfully. Unfortunately the same couldn't be said of her. After a while her back began to spasm and pull from leaning over him the way she was. She hesitated, then shifted her hips to perch on the very edge of the couch.

"Are you tired? You can stop." Garret's voice emerged gruff and husky.

"Just getting comfortable," she assured him as she returned to her ministrations. His winter-dry skin absorbed the fluid, so she added more massage oil, then kept her pressure and touch steady as she applied the last of the specialized oils she liked to use. Rosewood and lavender, sandalwood. The scents blended well together, a tantalizing, heady fragrance she associated with sleep.

Once more, Darcy ran her hands up to his neck, and across his back to his shoulders, upper arms and biceps until the muscles were completely lax beneath his skin. Finishing what she could of his arms with one of them scrunched up against the couch near his head, she returned to his back, her hands creating a friction she'd felt many times before, but never like this. She felt every tingle, the play of muscles and bone. The heat.

Hormones again. Had to be. Women were sexually charged beings during pregnancy, their bodies on overload. But it hadn't been a problem before now which meant it was…because of Garret? She tried to focus, gave herself another lecture about professionalism and hoped he didn't notice the slight hitch in her breathing. Still, she found herself pressing her knees together and once again thinking things she shouldn't be thinking about her host. Luckily Garret's breathing had eased. Had he fallen asleep? She wasn't sure, but it was definitely time to end the session.

She smoothed her hands over his oil-silken skin one last time, moving slowly so as not to disturb him. A portion of the sheet lay between the couch and his side, and she placed the body-warmed material over him. Normally she'd use damp, warm towels to let the oils "bake," but she'd improvise. Sheet in place, she rubbed her hands along his back to help create warmth through friction. Then she covered him with the lightweight blanket, as well, lingering over the task and knowing without a doubt that when she closed her eyes to sleep tonight she'd dream of Garret.

CHAPTER ELEVEN

GARRET AWOKE to the sound of laughter, throaty and feminine. Darcy. A smile formed on his lips before he opened his eyes. Muffled noises came from the kitchen, then Ethan's laugh joined Darcy's.

Huh?

He turned his head and squinted toward the clock on the electronics across from the couch. Nine-thirty. *Nine-thirty?* He hadn't slept that late in— Not in years. And on a couch?

Remembering the night before, he put both palms over his face and rubbed. When she'd started the massage everything had been okay. His headache had started to ease, his neck had stopped hurting. But then she'd sat beside him and it was like having a jolt of electricity zap him.

He didn't know if it was his abstinence of late, Darcy's touch or the oils, but he'd been hard instantly. His mind had filled with all of the ways they could make use of those oils, and his body had turned into a furnace. Every stroke made him want to roll over and do some touching of his own.

After reciting the alphabet—backward—then forcing himself to plow through legal briefs in his head, he'd resorted to faking sleep to end the torture.

Shrugging off the knowledge that he was one sick puppy to lust after a pregnant woman, he gave himself time to get his body under control and rose, donning his shirt along the way.

"There's Sleeping Beauty."

Ethan's tone mocked him from the stool where he sat as Garret entered the kitchen. He yawned and chose not to respond to the teasing. "When did you get home?"

"An hour ago. Good thing I didn't call, huh? You were dead to the world when I came in."

Darcy turned from the stove to smile at Garret. "I told you I could get you to sleep through the night."

Ethan raised a suspicious eyebrow, then sniffed the air. "What's that smell?"

He ignored his brother's question and Darcy's amused gaze, and focused on what she was cooking. His stomach growled. "Pancakes?"

"They're almost ready. You like them, don't you?"

"Love 'em. Do I have time for a quick shower?"

"Sure. Ten minutes?"

"I'm going to go get out of these scrubs." Ethan

stood and dogged Garret's steps all the way into the bedroom.

Once there, his older brother shut the door and leaned against it. "Are you *nuts?* I heard all about you rescuing some woman, but I didn't know you'd brought her home. Why did you?"

"The state of emergency?"

"Like that ever stopped anyone from getting on the roads. I made it home, didn't I?"

"You risking your neck is one thing. Taking a pregnant woman out there when she's already had false labor would be the ultimate in stupidity."

Ethan's gaze narrowed. "No, the ultimate in stupidity is having her here in the first place. Does Joss know you brought another woman home?"

Garret had meant to call her yesterday and tell her what was going on but each time he'd picked up the phone, he couldn't do it. He didn't want to upset her since there was nothing he could do about Darcy until the roads cleared, so he'd told himself the conversation could wait. Guilt stirred suggesting that had been a bad decision. "Darcy's not another woman."

"She sure as hell looks like one to me." Ethan's voice lowered even more. "When I heard she was pregnant, I pictured a house of a woman with a wedding ring on her finger and some guy named Bubba for a husband. Not a cute blonde who looks like she's simply hiding a basketball under her shirt and no ring in sight. So level with me. Are you in some kind of trouble?"

Garret struggled to grasp what his brother was asking. Sure, Joss was likely to freak a little when Garret told her about Darcy, but she'd get over it. "What do you mean?"

Ethan stared at him as if he'd lost his mind. "Darcy's baby? Are you the father?"

"*No*. Not even close." Garret grabbed jeans from a drawer, a fresh pullover from the closet. "How can you even think that? I only met Darcy Friday night."

"Harry's going to think the exact same thing and he's going to go ballistic."

"Darcy and I are two adults—strangers—in a snow crisis. Harry and Joss will understand." Garret frowned, well aware Harry wouldn't like Darcy's presence in his house. But Harry was his boss, not his father and—

And? Harry would be his father-in-law soon. Garret stalked back to the dresser and grabbed underwear. "Eth, she'd just been released from the hospital. What else could I do when all the motels were full?"

"Hey, I would've done the same, but my situation is different in a lot of ways." He smirked. "No one would've thought twice about me picking up a woman. You, on the other hand, are all wrapped up in commitment and obligation. This deal with Darcy looks bad so you'd better be prepared for the fallout. People like a good scandal and this has all the makings of one."

"You're right." Garret sighed, frustrated. He hated being the object of speculation and having people leap to the wrong conclusions. At the sharp nudge from his guilty conscience he had to admit that, under different circumstances, those conclusions wouldn't be far from the truth. He *was* attracted to Darcy. Damn, why hadn't he thought through the consequences of his actions more thoroughly? He usually was so careful. "Well, you're here now. That should smooth things over."

"You better hope it does."

"I'll take her to a motel as soon as a room opens up."

Ethan sniffed again, walking closer to where Garret stood. "What *is* that smell?" He stopped sniffing and jerked back in horror. "It's *you?*"

"It's…scented oils. Darcy's an aromatherapist." Heat crept into his face at Ethan's expression.

"Wait a minute. Are you telling me—"

"I had a monster headache. She wanted to repay me for helping her out."

"So she *massaged* you?" Ethan's gaze narrowed. "You were dead to the world when I got home. Are you sure you didn't get a roofie in your drink? You'd better hope photographs don't wind up on the Internet."

"She didn't drug me. Trust me when I say I didn't fall asleep for a long time afterward, all right? I pretended to be asleep so she'd stop."

Ethan squeezed his eyes shut with a groan. "This just keeps getting worse. She's *pregnant*."

"I know. I've already called myself every name you can think of and then some."

Ethan remained silent for a long moment. "For what it's worth, you wouldn't be the only guy getting a stiffy around her—if you don't look below her chest she's pretty cute."

Garret wanted to take Ethan to task for the statement but couldn't, not when he'd thought the same himself. "Just take it easy and don't give her a hard time, okay? Everything is fine."

But everything wasn't fine. *Screwed* didn't begin to cover the state of affairs he'd be in if his parents and Harry, not to mention Joss, misconstrued Darcy's presence. "I'm going to shower. Do me a favor and help her out in the kitchen. Without the attitude, please."

Ethan headed toward the door, but paused with his hand on the knob. "I understand why you picked her up. Even why you brought her home. You did the right thing. Just be careful. There are a lot of women who'd take one look at you and decide Junior could use a daddy."

DARCY BREATHED a sigh of relief as both Garret and Ethan left the kitchen. Breakfast had been a chore to get through with everyone pretending Ethan hadn't said anything to Garret about her being there. Did he seriously think his voice hadn't carried through the house? She hadn't made out every word, but the tone was clear. And the tension between them? Neither man would ever win an award for acting.

She blinked back ridiculous tears and plopped another plate on the counter beside the sink. It was stupid to be upset, but she couldn't help it. Who'd feel comfortable in a place where they knew they weren't welcome?

Garret cleared his throat from the doorway. "Sorry about that, I had to take the call. And there you go again. Leave those alone, I'll put them in the dishwasher."

Ready to escape, Darcy nodded. "Okay. I think I'm going to go try calling my mom again."

"Maybe this time you'll have some luck."

She made her way through the house, glaring at Ethan's closed door as she entered Garret's room. *Please, Mom, be home.* She grabbed the phone from the base and punched in her mother's number. This time after two rings, the recorded voice told her to leave a message.

"Mom, it's me again. Where are you? Call me as soon as you get my messages." She left the number once more and hung up. Almost immediately the phone rang. Her mother? She grabbed the receiver. "Hello?"

A slight pause sounded on the other end. "Hello. You must be a friend of Ethan's."

A friend of Ethan's? Interesting assumption. "Um, would you like to talk to him?"

"Oh, no, I'm calling for Garret. This is Jocelyn."

The way she said her name she might as well have attached *his girlfriend* onto the end. The pancakes threatened to revolt. Of course Garret had a girlfriend. He hadn't mentioned her, but apparently even white knights lied by omission. Not that she'd expected Garret to tell her everything about his life, but she'd told him about Stephen. He couldn't have *mentioned* a girlfriend? No wonder Ethan had followed Garret into the bedroom to *talk*. "Hold on a moment while I get Garret for you."

Darcy returned to the kitchen, holding the phone in front of her, the mouthpiece covered by her hand. And even though she was disappointed, she didn't want to cause him any trouble. Garret had been nice to her, gone above and beyond to help her. Just because he hadn't mentioned a girlfriend, well, typical guy. Why had she expected anything else?

"Garret, it's for you. Someone named Jocelyn." And there it was. Garret's expression turned guarded right before her eyes. He excused himself and, phone in hand, walked out.

Darcy palmed her stomach and made a face, staring down at her belly. "Come on, Marcus, the snow's letting up. Let's finish the dishes, then go pack."

GARRET ENTERED his office and shut the door behind him, feeling more guilt than the situation warranted. Nothing had happened between him and Darcy. "Joss, I've been meaning to call you."

"Oh? Sorry. I haven't been home."

Concern overrode guilt. "Where are you if not home?"

"The gallery. After you dropped me off Friday night, I heard about how bad the storm was going to be and packed a bag. I thought it better to be snowed in here where I can get some work done."

"You could've come home with me."

"And still not gotten any work done?" She laughed softly. "Besides, Tobias came by yesterday."

"He did?"

"Surprised me, too. He stayed for hours and helped me get things organized. And you'll never guess why he stopped by."

"Why?"

"He, um, brought the permit I needed to open."

Crap! Garret made a fist and punched his thigh. "Joss, I'm sorry. I can't believe I forgot the permit.

It completely slipped my mind." How many ways could he let this woman down?

"It's okay. I understand how busy you've been."

"That's no excuse."

"Hey, I'm a big girl. I know how things work. And I would've handled it myself if not for Tobias. I was floored by the gesture."

"Everything taken care of now?"

"Yes. Before he left we painted the far wall and hung some things. And we unpacked the displays for the pottery and assembled two of them. At this rate, I'll be able to open on time."

"Well, I'm glad you had help." He owed Tobe a day of golf, dinner. Something. "But I'm not crazy about you being there by yourself."

"I'm fine. So should I ask who Ethan's friend is? She's not another nurse from the hospital, is she? Didn't he learn his lesson about that after Daddy talked to him?"

"Ahh, actually she's not Ethan's friend." Garret inhaled and sighed. He couldn't put this off any longer. "Her name is Darcy Rhodes. I found her stranded by the side of the road Friday night. She was in labor."

"What?"

He told her the rest of the story. "I'm going to take her to a motel as soon as the roads are clear to travel. Until then I'm sleeping on the couch." He needed to clarify that, just in case Joss had doubts. "You're not upset because she's here, are you?"

"Of course not. Why would you ask that?"

"Just curious."

"It's sweet of you to look after her. Then again I'd expect nothing less. You've always liked playing hero."

Playing hero? "What do you mean?"

"Garret, you know you like fixing everything. Your family. The hospital. This is no different. Your second-child characteristics are very strong. It's very heroic and very admirable. That's a good thing."

Then why did she make it sound like a flaw? Because he hadn't remembered the permit? "Ethan thought you'd be upset."

"Yes, well, Ethan's experiences with women fighting over his attentions at the hospital would make him think that. But no, I'm not upset. For pity's sake, you just said she's how far along? If you'd left her by the side of the road, I'd have been horrified. I understand completely, Garret."

Her words rang with truth. She wasn't jealous, wasn't upset. In fact, it seemed as though Joss didn't mind at all. While he knew it was juvenile of him, it bothered him that she wasn't more troubled. He'd care plenty if Joss took another man home with her.

"Make sure you call the hotels before you leave this afternoon. There were so many power outages

I heard the companies brought in extra crews and they're staying in the area."

"I'll do that."

"Good. Now I'd better go. I've got to call Daddy and check in before he calls out the National Guard. Take care of your guest and let me know how things go. Bye."

Just like that the phone clicked in his ear. No "I love you," no nothing. Just "Bye." Shouldn't she be the slightest bit jealous? Have asked more questions? Even Ethan had issued a brotherly warning about Darcy. Shouldn't his girlfriend be a little more curious?

He pressed the button on the phone and set it aside. He and Joss hadn't spent more than a few hours in each other's company the entire month. And most of that time they had spent was surrounded by his family and hers on Christmas day.

She trusts you. Be glad she's not upset. Then you'd be kissing up trying to make amends.

Garret got back to work and was nose deep reading a deposition when the phone rang. Ahh, here it was. Joss had thought about things and was calling him back. "Hello?"

"Garret, what the hell is going on?"

He stilled. Had Joss called her father with her complaints instead of voicing them to him? What kind of behavior was that? "Sir?"

"I just got a call from a board member who said there are ten-foot snowdrifts in the parking lot."

He switched mental gears. *That's* why Harry was calling? "There's a lot of snow out there, Harry. They were told to pile it on the back lots farthest from the entrances."

"I don't want it there at all!"

He gritted his teeth, his hand gripping the phone tight. "It has to go somewhere. When they scrape off the parking lot because *we* want the spaces clear, where are they supposed to put it? They can't put it back in the air." Did Harry not have any sense?

Harry hem-hawed and grumbled for a moment. "Fine, but if I go down there to check things out and there's a snow pile on any of the front lots, that team is history. Fired! Do you understand me?"

"Yessir." Garret rubbed his eyes and pinched the bridge of his nose. So much for Darcy's massage.

"Jocelyn called, too."

He braced himself.

"I don't approve of her staying in that rat-trap building, son. Why she had to set up shop in the old part of town, I'll never know."

"I, uh, think rent had a lot to do with it."

"It's a waste of time and money. You need to take her in hand, Garret, and the only way you're going to do it is if you put a ring on her finger. What are you waiting for?"

He smiled wearily. Yet another jab. Joss could've been more interested in him, but at least she hadn't told her father about Darcy. Ethan was right. If Harry got wind of Darcy's presence, however innocent, his temper would blow sky-high and the pressure would really be on. "She's fine. The security system is top-notch."

"If she had a home and family to take care of she wouldn't be going so far to entertain herself."

"She likes art, Harry, and she's good at what she does. You should be proud of her accomplishments."

Harry grumbled a bit longer about the hospital and Joss "wasting money." Garret hated that Harry couldn't see how great his daughter was. But the only way he would have was if she had been born a son.

"Go take care of business, Garret. I'm counting on you to keep maintenance and my daughter on track."

"Have a good day, Harry." Garret hung up and leaned his head against the office chair, palming his face with both hands and rubbing hard.

Harry would make Garret's life a living hell if he didn't propose to Joss soon. He loved her, cared for her. Could see himself spending the rest of his life with her. They had a solid, good relationship.

So what *was* he waiting for? Why did the idea of forever with Joss seem so unsatisfying? Why wasn't he eager to make their relationship permanent?

And maybe the fact that he avoided probing into the answers to those questions told him all he needed to know.

CHAPTER TWELVE

THE NEXT MORNING Toby entered Garret's office in a piss-poor mood. What kind of friend lusted after his best friend's soon-to-be fiancée? Not a good one, that's for sure.

"What's wrong with you?"

Garret sat in his standard position—phone glued to his ear with a pile of paper in front of him and pen in hand. A workaholic at his best.

Ignoring the phone since Garret was doing the same, Toby got right to the point. "Jocelyn needs help at the gallery. I think she's overwhelmed trying to get ready for the opening. Did you go help her this weekend?"

Garret tugged at his tie and shook his head. "No, I couldn't get out. The roads didn't open up until late last night."

Like any cop in the area would ticket a Tulane. "I made it okay. I did some stuff for her."

"She told me." Jerking to attention, Garret spoke into the phone. "I'm on hold for Benjamin

Thomas. Yes, I would like to leave a message, thank you."

Toby approached Garret's desk and perused the surface, reaching out to grab a picture of Jocelyn before hesitating and picking up the one next to it. Garret's family was gathered around one of his mother's Christmas trees, Jocelyn included. And right there in full color he saw the way Jocelyn and Garret complimented each other—her sleek blond up-do and insanely expensive-looking red dress the perfect foil for Garret's jet-black hair and suit. A debutante and one of Beauty's founding families' sons. Go figure.

"Hey, sorry about that." Garret hung up and settled back in his chair. "The board meeting was postponed and one guy's already in transit, so we're trying to track him down before he gets here and has a fit. And thanks for helping Joss out. Especially with the permit."

"I thought you'd taken care of it for her."

A disgusted expression flickered over Garret's face. "I was going to but I forgot about it. The mess with the buyout has me forgetting my own name. I owe you one."

"You don't owe me for the permit." If anything he owed Garret, seeing as how Toby had enjoyed the time with Jocelyn way more than he should have. "But you do owe me for not making our racquetball slot this morning. Where were you?"

Garret fiddled with the pen and cleared his throat. "I tried to call."

"I got the message when I got back to the locker room. Don't tell me your twenty-two-inch wheels couldn't take a little slush."

Making a face, Garret motioned for Toby to shut the door behind him.

He did as requested. "What's wrong?"

"I picked up a woman who wrecked Friday night. After the hospital released her, I drove her to the motels but they were full so…I took her home with me. She spent the weekend."

Toby stared at Garret, the urge to deck him so strong his knuckles cracked. Garret picked up strangers when he had a woman like Jocelyn waiting for him to make the next move? "Did you *cheat* on her?" Toby barely got the words out. Not because he actually thought Garret *had* cheated on Jocelyn but because he was shocked to his core that, in a sick and twisted way, he wanted it to be true. Why? So he'd have a chance with Jocelyn?

Garret glared at him. "Of course not! It was nothing like that. And I've already talked to Joss about it, so stop being an ass."

He'd been Garret's friend for over half his life. Toby knew Garret wasn't like that. But if Garret had cheated on her— What? Toby would tell her? Be happy about it? What kind of friend was *that?*

"Who is she?"

"No one you know. She's just traveling through town."

"She could be anyone. One of those women who go home with a guy, drugs him then opens the door for the boyfriend so they can rob him before murdering the guy."

"You've been watching too much *Dateline*."

"Ethan wasn't at the house the whole weekend. I saw him in the cafeteria when I went down to get something for Maria. Which means you—" he pointed a finger at Garret "—were at the house alone with this woman. What did you do with her for hours on end?"

"I did exactly what you gave me such a hard time about the other night—I worked. Darcy rested and hung out. She'd just been in an accident—and she's pregnant. Why is this such a big deal to you?"

"It's not." Toby raked his fingers through his hair and moved to the door of Garret's office. "You didn't say she was pregnant." Like that made a difference? Toby had to get out of there. Liking Jocelyn was one thing, admiring her from afar, fine. But this feeling was more than *like*. And Garret was his best friend.

"Tobe, nothing happened."

Maybe not, but a lot had happened in the past five minutes. Garret had to propose to Jocelyn soon.

With his ring on her finger, she really *would* be off-limits—that was a boundary Toby wouldn't cross. Ever. But until that happened, he had to stay away from her—them—altogether. It was only right.

"What's with you today? You look ready to self-combust."

He gripped the knob, wishing he could rip it off and throw it. "I thought maybe you'd...done something you shouldn't have."

"I didn't."

A look flashed over Garret's face, though. Guilt? Toby turned and leaned against the door. "You sure?"

Garret avoided his gaze and stood to pace to the window. "Nothing happened."

"But?"

"But how do I know Joss is the one?" Garret glanced over his shoulder at him. "Don't go mentioning this to your mother or sister but— You nailed me for not giving Joss the ring, and this is why. How do I know she's the one?"

"You're having second thoughts? You think it's a mistake to marry Jocelyn?"

"Not a mistake. Joss would never be a mistake. She's as perfect as a woman can come but..."

Toby struggled to find the right words, the things guys were supposed to say in situations like this. Somehow they all sounded false in his head while he silently cheered getting an opportunity to pursue

Jocelyn. "You've just got cold feet. It's hard for a guy to think that he's giving up the field." He knew Garret was a stand-up guy who cared for and honored the woman he was with. If Toby thought for a second that Garret used women when they were convenient, that his feelings for Jocelyn weren't sincere, Toby would consider her free for the chase. But Garret wasn't like that and Toby had to respect their relationship.

"You're right. Cold feet. What else could it be, right? I love her, why shouldn't I marry her?"

Toby opened the door. "I can't think of a single reason."

Not one he could say out loud, that is.

GARRET STARED out the window a long time after Toby left. Once his engagement to Joss became official, his mother and Joss's would go off the deep end planning the wedding. It would be the first in the family and sure to create a fuss. He'd be asked to discuss parties and seating arrangements, colors and flowers. Stuff he didn't have the time or desire to mess with. This was exactly why people eloped.

A soft knock sounded on his door. "Come in."

"Hey, what's going on?" Joss asked as she stepped into his office wearing a sleek blue pantsuit that matched her eyes. "I saw Tobias getting in one of the elevators. He looked angry."

Maybe he needed a little reminder of the spark between them. Maybe it had been so long since they'd had sex that he was forgetting the way they connected. He crossed the room and pulled her into his arms, lowering his head for a kiss. Their lips brushed, but when he tried to deepen the caress, she pulled away.

"Where's Daddy?"

"Not due in for another hour." He stepped close once more and kissed her cheek, nuzzled his way toward her mouth, but sighed when he felt her straight-arming him.

"Garret, come on."

"I'm trying to."

She shook her head at him and wouldn't meet his gaze. "You know how Daddy feels about public affection and appearances."

"We're in my office." He reached behind her and shut the door. "Private. Kiss me."

Glancing over her shoulder toward the door one last time, she obediently raised herself on tiptoe and pressed her mouth to his, her lips parting, but after a quick, chaste taste, she broke contact.

"How's the woman you rescued?"

Garret fought his frustration with her lack of response and tried not to think about precisely how long it had been. "She's fine. She's here in the hospital, actually. She has a follow-up this morning."

"Good."

Joss started to move away but he snuggled her deeper into the embrace. "Why don't I take an early lunch? We can lock the door—"

"And have Daddy barge in and interrupt us?"

Good point. "I'll take a break and come by the gallery instead."

"I have deliveries scheduled this afternoon."

"The house?"

"Mother's home and neither one of us has time to drive to your place."

He stared down at her. "Are you sure that's it?"

"What do you mean?"

"You won't stay with me because you feel un-comfortable at the house with Ethan, don't want to risk the gallery or here. Joss—"

She stiffened. "Don't get that look. I came by to say hello, not to argue or have a quickie. Does everything always come have down to sex?"

"We're not talking about sex, we're talking about us."

"But you're making it about sex." She backed away from him.

"Joss—"

"Forget it. I'm PMSing, all right? I didn't want to be blunt, but I'm moody and there it is. I've got to go."

"Don't leave angry."

A knock sounded on the other side of the door.

What now? "I want to finish this," he told her. "Don't leave. Whoever it is can wait."

"I don't want to be late." She opened the door so abruptly she surprised his father on the other side. Alan Tulane took a step back, his gaze moving between the two of them. "Am I interrupting?"

"No, not at all. Goodbye, Garret."

"Joss—"

She gave his father a strained smile before she headed out the door, the sharp click of her heels loud on the tiled floor.

His father's eyebrows rose. "Bad time?"

"Depends on the perspective."

"Could it have something to do with this woman I'm hearing you rescued?"

Garret sighed. "Maybe. Probably. Joss said she wasn't mad about her staying, but—"

"I wondered about that. I heard on the news that the hotels were overflowing. She spent the weekend at the house with you?"

"And Ethan. Don't look at me like that, Dad. She's almost eight months pregnant. What else was I supposed to do? I couldn't leave her in the lobby."

"No, I suppose not." Alan made a face. "Unfortunately, I've learned women can get upset over innocent situations, and I have a feeling you're going to have to make up for this with Joss. Send her some flowers, take her to dinner. A little romance will go a long way."

Garret nodded his agreement. "I'll do that. We've both been working a lot lately and haven't seen much of each other."

"Then that's probably it. She's feeling neglected. Everything else all right?"

"Yeah." He indicated the brown paper sack his father carried. "Are those my cookies Mom promised?"

His dad tossed the sack to him with a smile. "Don't eat them all at once," he said, like he always had when they were kids.

"I know." He pulled out one and consumed half of it in a single bite.

Chuckling, his father headed out. "I've got patients to see, much to your mother's upset."

"Still wanting you to retire, huh?"

"I'm considering cutting my time down. I don't have the energy I used to."

"Are you feeling okay?"

"Fine, fine. Oh, and son?"

Garret tucked the cookie into the side of his mouth. "What?"

"If the girl is trustworthy and safe—"

"She is," he said, knowing exactly who his father referred to. "I'd stake my life on it."

"That's high praise coming from you."

"It's true. She pitched in all weekend, trying to make up for us taking her in. The dad's out of the picture, too. She didn't say much about her finances but she's worried about getting her car fixed and getting settled in Indiana before she gives birth. I took it to mean things are tight."

A medical doctor for nearly forty years, his father sighed. "Always sad when that's the case. Expectant mothers shouldn't be stressed, especially so close to delivery. You call Nick?"

"Yeah." He saw the question in his father's eyes and wished things were different. "He sounded good. He said Matt was excited about the snow and they were getting ready to go sledding."

"He's a good dad."

"So are you."

His father shoved a hand into his pocket. "I've made more than my share of mistakes. Still, I'm sure Nick appreciates the business."

"Dad—"

"You're a good judge of character, Garret. Always have been. If you think this woman is safe and she needs a place to stay while her car is fixed, why don't you try your grandmother? Gram could probably use the company. It might also get Joss off your back—and your mother off mine when she hears what's going on."

That was the best idea he'd heard all day. Darcy

would be safe; he wouldn't worry about her or wonder why he'd reacted so strongly to her. And neither Joss, Harry or his mother could complain. "I can't believe I didn't think of that. Great idea."

His father tapped his temple with a finger. "Marriage smarts. Don't forget to call the florist," he said as a parting shot.

Rounding the desk, Garret dialed the local florist and requested a bouquet be delivered that afternoon. After that he punched in the garage's number.

"Make it quick," Nick said. "Business is good at the moment."

"Hello to you, too, little brother. Did you have a chance to tow the VW I called about Saturday?"

"Just got it in. The driver did a number on the passenger side. The fender collapsed into the wheel, but I don't know yet if it damaged the axle."

"How long and how much?" He could practically see Nick running the numbers through his head. The guy was a whiz at math. "Depends on parts. If that piece is damaged, it'll be expensive regardless. She a friend of yours?"

"You could say that. Pregnant, too. She's alone and in between jobs."

Nick whistled softly. "That's rough." A pause came over the line. "Let me see what I can do. Maybe I can find some junker parts. If I can, that'll cut the cost down considerably. I won't put anything substandard on there, but it might take longer to get it since I'm not ordering it straight from the factory."

"I'd appreciate whatever you can do to help." Garret hesitated. He and Nick talked as though they were strangers or business acquaintances. Not family. He hated the distance between them. How had things deteriorated to this point? "Give me a call when you hear something?"

"Why don't I just contact her?"

"I, uh, don't have a number for her offhand."

"You can call and leave it with Sara when you get it."

So Nick wouldn't have to talk to him? "Okay, sure. Nick, listen, thanks for the help. Maybe we can get together for dinner sometime at the Grille?"

"Maybe. See you around."

Garret hung up the phone, angry with his parents and Nick for being so stubborn. And angry with himself for letting anything come between family members. His disagreement with Joss and his resentment toward Harry with his frequent absences that tripled Garret's already overwhelming workload piled in along with Toby's censure to create a mountain of dissatisfaction with his life. He just needed a break.

His thoughts strayed to Darcy's massage Saturday night and how relaxing it had been. Well, relaxing until his body had gone into hyperdrive at her proximity and touch.

Had Darcy had her appointment? Was the baby okay? He glanced at his watch, then stood. His guilt pricked at him but he shrugged it off. His own girl-friend wasn't concerned about Darcy, so why should he worry about wanting to see her again? That's what friends did.

CHAPTER THIRTEEN

DARCY SMOOTHED her shirt over her stomach and waited impatiently for Garret's brother to pick up the phone.

"This is Nick. Can I help you?"

She twisted the wire phone cord around her finger. "Hi, Nick, my name is Darcy Rhodes. I believe your brother Garret talked to you about my car? A Volkswagen? I was wondering if you could give me an estimate on the repair cost and timetable?"

"I just got off the phone with Garret. We're looking at two weeks or more. I'll have to get back with you on the estimate. I'm going to call around to see if I can get a better price. Do you have rental coverage?"

"No." She groaned, then winced at her manners. "Sorry, I didn't mean to sound ungrateful. It's just— Don't worry that I won't pay you or anything. I will, I promise. But if I'm going to be here that long waiting on my car to be repaired, I'll have to find a part-time job."

"What do you do?"

She hesitated, then told him and waited for the snarky comment that sometimes began with "Oh, yeah?" and ended with "Well, maybe for a little extra you'll massage my—"

"Oh, yeah?"

Don't say it!

"You're certified?"

The question stumped her. "Uh, yes. Yes, I am."

"I've been looking for a massage therapist for my gym. Maybe we could work out something that way. You interested?"

Another white knight? "Seriously? That would be—" She fumbled for a word to express her gratitude. "That would be great. Thank you." After everything Garret had told her about Nick, she had no qualms working for him. And Nick had already proven himself by not degrading her profession.

"I'll get back with you later today and we'll see if we can't work out a deal. Sound good?"

She closed her eyes in relief. The women in this town were crazy for not scarfing the Tulane men up. "It sounds perfect but— My cell phone is in my car and I'm not sure where I'll be later. Perhaps I could call you when I'm settled?"

"Great. Talk to you soon."

Darcy murmured goodbye and hung up, relieved and worried at the same time. Her back ached, and she pressed her hands against the base, rubbing.

"You okay?" Garret asked, walking toward her where she stood at a pay phone.

She'd asked about his schedule this morning on the way to the hospital, so she knew he'd ducked out of a series of meetings to come see her. "I'm fine. What are you doing here?"

Garret stopped in front of her and, the way it had every time he stood so near, her heart picked up its pace. He was so handsome. Especially when he looked at her with that expression of tender concern and— No, he wasn't interested. Not any more than the average guy would be interested in a very rounded, pregnant woman. Sex appeal? Yeah, right. Somehow she'd managed to stumble upon a genuinely nice man.

"The meeting ended early and the other one was canceled. I came to find you and let you know you're not going to a motel."

"I'm not?"

"No, come on. You can tell me what the doc said on the way."

Minutes later Darcy was seated in the Escalade beside Garret getting grilled on the ob-gyn's every word.

They left the hospital parking lot and drove around the outer belt of road surrounding the area. Lined with bare trees and snowbanks, the houses had been made commercial. Now they were quaint-looking doctor's offices, a law firm, three florists and a health food store.

And there it was again. That flash of a smile, the look, and—a firm nod? "Why are you nodding?"

"Because it makes me feel even stronger about you not staying alone while you're here."

"Dr. Clyde said I'm fine. I just need to take it easy for a few days and then I can get back to work. My blood pressure is up, but she thinks it'll go down once things are settled."

He turned and traveled down a quiet street. On the right was a large sign. *The Village.* Garret slowed and turned again just in front of it, waving at the guard at the gate. They passed small, two-family homes with one-car garages on either side of the houses, then several buildings two and three stories tall.

"You brought me to stay at a *nursing* home?"

Still going, Garret chuckled and parked in front of one of the three-story buildings. "That's only one section. You're staying in the condos."

"Weren't those condos back there?"

"Those are townhomes. They require more maintenance. The condos are maintenance free."

"Garret, I appreciate the gesture, honestly, but this looks out of my price range. Would you mind taking me to the motel?"

Garret stretched one hand across the interior of the SUV and gave her palm a reassuring squeeze.

"Trust me. This is better than any motel room, and it'll ease my mind knowing you're safe."

She stared into his dark, moss-colored eyes and found herself wishing the impossible. It was scary how easily he reassured her. She was aware of him on so many levels.

Overactive hormones. They'd brought more than one woman low over the years.

"Don't move. I'll grab your suitcase and come get you. It's still icy." Her hand tingled long seconds after he'd released it.

Inside the building, Garret removed his warm palm from her elbow and knocked on a door. Someone else was in there? Absurdly nervous, she tugged at her maternity blouse, fluffed her hair where her coat had crushed it and tried to hide her misgivings.

The door opened. "Garret." An older woman greeted them. Seventysomething, she had jet-black hair streaked with silver and cut in a sleek style. She wore black pants and a black sweater with dangling earrings Darcy knew had to be diamonds. The only other splash of color came in the intricately woven silver wrap the woman had tied loosely around her shoulders.

Darcy watched as Garret bent to drop a kiss on the woman's wrinkled cheek. Whoever she was she'd aged well.

"You look beautiful as always."

"And you're overcompensating for the fact that you work so much you never come see me even though I'm practically right next door."

Garret looked embarrassed by the chiding statement. "I'm here now, aren't I? And I brought the company I promised you."

Darcy bit back a gulping moan when the woman turned her shrewd gaze on her.

"You must be Darcy. Garret's told me all about you, dear."

She wished she could say the same. "It's nice to meet you…" She looked toward Garret for help.

Garret appeared boyish as he wrapped his arm around the woman's shoulders and grinned. "Darcy, allow me to introduce you to Gram, otherwise known as Rosetta Tulane, my grandmother. Gram, Darcy Rhodes."

He'd brought her to stay with his *grandmother?* She pasted a smile on her lips. "It's very nice to meet you."

The woman's gaze seemed to take her measure, hesitating only briefly on her stomach. "Likewise, dear. Why are we standing here? Come in out of the drafty hall."

The temperature in the building was anything but drafty. Garret prodded her inside with a hand at her back, and Darcy followed his grandmother into the condo, waiting while Garret brought in her suitcase.

"I'll get us something to drink. Garret, take Darcy's coat and make her comfortable."

"Yes, ma'am."

As soon as Rosetta was out of sight, Darcy rounded on him. "How could you?"

"How could I what?"

"Not *warn* me." Darcy made sure to keep her voice low. "Your grandmother? You should've told me I was going to meet her. I would've—" What?

He tilted his head to one side, amusement lighting his features. "You look fine. What does it matter?"

Good question. It shouldn't matter. It wasn't as though she was a girlfriend Garret was bringing home to introduce. That position had already been filled. She just hated that Garret's grandmother's first impression was of her homeless, jobless and pregnant. "I can't stay here, that's why. And why on earth would she even agree to let me?"

"Because I asked her. She knows your situation with the car and the storm, and she wants to help."

"She doesn't even know me. *You* don't know me, not really."

Garret grabbed her hands from where they rubbed her stomach in fast strokes. "I know enough. Now calm down or the contractions will start again. What's the problem?"

He was right so she tried to calm her nerves. His

grandmother was probably a lovely woman, but she couldn't imagine staying with a stranger. This wasn't a snowstorm emergency. "I don't want to be any more trouble and— Do you not remember what I said about not accepting charity? A motel is fine."

"Nonsense, dear." Rosetta appeared behind them, a tray in her hands. "A woman so late in her pregnancy shouldn't be alone, especially if she's having problems. And it wouldn't be appropriate for you to continue staying with my bachelor grandsons," she told her pointedly. "This is a perfect solution until your car is repaired. You must think of the future. You'll need to provide for the baby, not spend your money on overpriced lodging. You'll be much more comfortable here, too."

Darcy realized Garret had stood there the entire time holding her hands in his, and she yanked them away, praying his grandmother hadn't noticed.

"I'm quite excited about your staying here. I lived at home when I went to college and I imagine this will be like having a roommate in one of those— Oh, what are they called?"

"A dorm, Gram. They're called dormitories."

"Yes, that." She set the tray on the coffee table, smoothing the ends of her silver wrap back into place when she settled herself on the couch. "Please don't be angry with my grandson, Darcy. I really do want to help. Things get a bit lonely here this time of year when so many of the residents go south to warmer areas. I have a spare bedroom to offer and insist you think about your little one. Perhaps you would consider your room and board payment for being my companion? I'd love the company."

Darcy glanced at Garret again, and found him awaiting her response. "Well…"

"Come sit down, dear. Let's get to know one another. Garret, you go to work and stop by again this evening. Darcy will have made her decision by then, and if she still wants to go to a motel you can take her. How does that sound for a compromise?"

Darcy knew there was little choice to be made. Garret had disrupted his schedule enough for her, and Rosetta had a point. Her options were to stay here with someone who seemed like a very nice woman, or a hotel she couldn't afford. She took in the homey interior of the condo, then studied Garret's and Rosetta's expressions. "That sounds good. Thank you."

Garret squeezed her shoulder on the way out the door, standing close and smelling heavenly. "Have fun," he murmured, his breath sending a shiver over her. "Just remember to rest. Gram can be a party animal."

PAIN STABBED through Jocelyn as quickly as the box cutter had sliced into her hand. She gasped and swore, dropping the utility knife and then jumping back when it clattered onto the floor at her feet.

"Careful, you don't want Daddy to hear you."

Pressing on the cut to try to dull the pain, she turned and saw Tobias weaving his way through the boxes and crates that had arrived today. Pottery and glassware carefully packed, a sculpture from Spain. All she was missing were the pieces by a Montana artist she desperately wanted to showcase. Why wouldn't the silly man call her back?

Tobias's gaze dropped to her hand. "What the—" He hurried around the last of the obstacles and grabbed a towel she'd been using to dust the pieces after she removed them from their packing. "Give me your hand."

"That's dirty."

"It's better than letting that bleed." He took the decision away from her and wrapped the towel around it, pressing firmly.

"What are you doing here?"

His jaw locked. "I came to look at some office space that's available and thought I'd drop by and see if your help arrived. Looks like I'm just in time."

"Office space? Why are you—"

"It's a long story."

Joss lifted her hand and placed it over his. "What happened?"

His scowl deepened. "I turned in my notice."

"What? You've been with Wellington, Wellington and Deere for years. How could you quit when you're up for a…? Oh, Tobias."

His hair hung over his forehead as he stared down at their tangled hands. "They gave the partnership to someone else." He smirked, but she could tell it was for show. One glance revealed his hurt, the anger rolling off him. He had every right to be angry, too.

Mr. Wellington was one of her father's friends, but she knew him well enough to know he played favorites and often made promises he had no intention of ever keeping, all in the name of business. "Are you looking for office space to open your own practice?"

"Maybe. I don't know. I'm going to check into things and I thought I might contact a headhunter."

She stiffened. "You can't leave town."

"Why not?"

"Because…your family would be upset. Garret, too. You had a bad day, Tobias, but you don't want to leave."

"What about you?"

Jocelyn swallowed, the sound audible in the otherwise quiet building. "What do you mean?"

"Would you care if I left?"

CHAPTER FOURTEEN

"OF COURSE." She tried, oh, how she tried, but his lion eyes wouldn't let her look away. "I know you're angry but—"

"Why?" he insisted.

"Garret—"

"I'm not talking about Garret. Would *you* care if I left?"

What did he expect her to say? "You're a good friend, Tobias. If you hadn't helped me with the permit, I wouldn't be able to open."

"In other words, I'm the go-to boy when Garret is busy."

"Of course not! I meant— What do you want me to say?" The words came out sharper than she'd intended.

"Nothing. I don't expect you to say anything. I was just wondering if you'd actually have an opinion of your own."

The cut on her hand hurt like crazy but Tobias's comment caused more pain. She had plenty of opinions, plenty of brains and— "I'd care. What kind of space are you looking for? There's an empty office above the gallery here."

Joss turned away and stooped to pick up the box cutter. Her father would be furious. Garret wouldn't care, of course, but her father—

"You want to rent me the space upstairs?" He sounded surprised. No wonder. She wasn't sure why she'd offered.

"I merely mentioned it's available," she corrected, trying to backpedal and not doing a good job of it. "It's sitting there and the rent would help meet my payment. Never mind. You obviously aren't interested."

"I'm interested."

She closed her eyes. "I should probably mention it to Garret before—"

"Can I see it?"

"Now?"

"Why mention me renting it if I don't like it? Show it to me, and then I'll help you unpack all of this and put it wherever it needs to go. I don't have anything else to do at the moment. Wellington told me to get the hell out so I packed up my stuff and left."

"You said you gave notice."

"I lied." He shoved his big hands into his pockets. "It sounded better than saying I told him where he could stick his partnership and got fired."

"Good for you." She swallowed, her heart beating a little too fast. Why should she care that Tobias told Wellington off? Why should she feel proud of him? But she did. Because she wanted to do the same with her father. Wanted to stand up to him and people like Mr. Wellington, prove their meanness and hatefulness would come back to haunt them because the people they disregarded would rise above their sad behavior. "Let me get the keys and a Band-Aid."

"I'll come with you."

Too aware of Tobias following her, she entered the office and grabbed the first-aid kit. While she sprayed the cut with antiseptic, he opened a Band-Aid. Did his hands tremble, just a little? Or was that hers? Finally the protective strip was in place and they were on their way upstairs in the old-fashioned elevator.

"So…have you talked to Garret today?"

"Earlier, yes." Why hadn't she noticed how slow the elevator was before? "Briefly." Finally the elevator settled into place. "Here we are." The third floor spread out in front of them. "The area is only about two thousand square feet. I doubt it's what you're looking for but—"

"It's perfect."

"Oh." She watched Tobias look around the area, his big body moving with surprising masculine grace. Strong lines, the proud tilt of his head. He'd be a hard man to sketch but she'd love to tackle the challenge. A bronze nude would—

She blinked, her heart beating out of rhythm. She had no business, no business at all, looking at Tobias like that. Why had she? She loved Garret. But the last few times they'd been together she'd left the encounters feeling frustrated and uneasy. It was silly, nothing more than stress. She loved Garret, and how many couples didn't share one iota of love between them? They could be happy, *would* be happy if he ever proposed. It was silly to let absurd, inconsequential things irritate her the way they seemed to be doing of late.

But she couldn't help it. She hated the way Garret rubbed his chin anytime he was sitting still, and his awful taste in movies that lacked even the most basic plot. More guns and action did not a blockbuster make. And art? How could anyone *not* appreciate art on some level?

"Are you planning on doing anything with it soon?" Tobias's gaze narrowed on her. "What's wrong? What were you thinking about?"

Her mind scrambled for an appropriate topic. "Rosetta's birthday party. It's coming up."

"Not for a month." Tobias moved close. "Jocelyn…" He ran a hand over his face, and she knew he didn't want to say whatever was on his mind. "You and Garret are bound to have some rough spots. You just have to stick it out and be strong."

Stick it out? Be strong? Why did she always have to be the one to give in? Conform? What about Garret? Realizing Tobias knew nothing of her thoughts, and the topic probably had more to do with Garret's actions over the weekend, she sighed. "If this is about the pregnant woman he rescued, I'm not worried."

A muscle ticked in his jaw. "Sure about that? You looked worried."

"Tobias, he's Garret. He's just doing what he does best, what he's always done. One of the ladies from The Village stopped by this morning to congratulate me on snagging such a hero, and then proceeded to grill me on what I knew about the woman staying with Rosetta. Think he'd take a mistress there? I'm *not* worried."

As she spoke she felt, saw, his attention shift lower. To her mouth? A low throb unfurled in her stomach. "Garret and I are fine. We're both busy. Besides, I couldn't plan a wedding now, anyway."

"Some people think that's what wedding planners are for. And your mother and his would handle everything if you'd let them."

"I'd want to plan my own wedding."

"Does that mean you're going to turn Garret down if he asks?"

"No! Of course not. How could I after all this time?"

"You just said you didn't have time to get married. Surely you wouldn't do it simply because your father wants it to happen?"

She released a hollow laugh. Where was he going with this? "I'd make time. And I'm sure everyone in town has heard Daddy's views on when and where and how Garret and I should get married, but I wouldn't do it unless I wanted to."

"Do you?"

"Any woman would be nuts not to want to marry Garret." That wasn't an answer and they both knew it. He watched her too closely, made her afraid to blink, to move, because if she did, he'd see the truth. The doubts. "Really, Tobias, why all the questions? Do you doubt my sincerity?"

"I've known you long enough to know you generally do what your father says."

"Not always. He didn't want me opening this gallery and I'm still doing it. And that's the second time you've indicated you *think* you know me better than you do. How is that possible when you've always disliked me and kept your distance as if you're afraid to be near me?"

Her comment spurred him to action. Jaw rigid as though he ground his teeth into nubs, Tobias took slow, deliberate steps toward her. Joss backed up, the trembling inside her growing.

"I'm not afraid to be near you. Why would you think that?"

"You always seem…uncomfortable around me."

He took in her quivering stance with a sweep of his gaze. "The same is true of you."

"Only because you glare at me all the time."

"With good reason. Maybe *I'm* uncomfortable because I don't like thinking of you as a sacrificial lamb willing to sell herself for a ring and a bank account to make Daddy happy."

"How *dare* you!"

"Admit it. Harry wants a toehold in the Tulane family, and you're his ticket. Am I wrong?"

Her back hit the wall. She swallowed at the abrupt end of her retreat and hated the expression of superiority on his face. "Is that why you're friends with Garret? Because *you're* using him?"

She knew in an instant she'd said the wrong thing, but it was too late to take the words back. Tobias closed the remaining distance between them, not stopping until he stood so close she could see the gold flecks in the burnt sienna in his eyes, such a beautiful amber. Garret was more handsome by far, but Tobias—

He braced a hand on the wall beside her head, his body blocking her escape. "He's going to ask you to marry him soon, and it kills me to think that you might say yes just to make your father happy."

The words came out an angry growl, and a sizzle of excitement raced down her spine. This was the man she'd seen in the teenager she'd known. Angry, driven to right injustices, determined to protect those he loved and valued as friends. *Passionate*. What would it be like to be the object of that passion?

Scalding heat rushed into her cheeks.

"You want to know what I think? I think you've avoided Garret for months because it's starting to dawn on you that there's more to life than always doing what your daddy says and being Garret's eye candy. First it was charity work and finishing your art degree. You even used Garret's work schedule as an excuse. Now it's the gallery."

"You don't know what you're talking about. Garret and I are both busy and my life is none of your business. Why do you care?"

"Because he's my friend. Because he never treated me like I was second best and I'd hate to see him wind up in a second-rate marriage."

Staring at Tobias, she lost the ability to breathe.

Was it true? Heaven knew her father would overlook a lot of things, but he'd never forgive her if she ruined her future with Garret and the running of his precious hospital.

"What's wrong with me?"

"What do you mean?"

"I don't know what's *wrong* with me," she said

again. "Garret is… He's wonderful. He's smart and kind and giving. So handsome." She held eye contact with him, pleading with him to understand. "But sometimes he drives me *crazy*," she admitted, her voice shaking. "He sings these godawful ditties that don't make sense, and he always has a pen in his hand that he won't stop *clicking*. And when he kisses me, it's like he's afraid I'm going to break. I *won't* break. I'm not some kind of china doll too expensive to play with and I want— I want *more!*"

She stared up at him, horrified at what she'd said. And to Garret's best friend? But Tobias listened to her every word. As if he heard her, *really heard her.*

Breathing hard, she dropped her gaze to his mouth and she didn't stop to think of the consequences. Desire singed her veins, the same desire reflected in his eyes. In the flaring of his nostrils when he realized her intent. But he didn't move away. No, as she flung herself against him and pressed her mouth over his, he groaned, but he didn't back away.

A second, that's all he gave her before he took control. Not a soft gentle kiss but one that rocked her head back with the force of it. She moaned when his tongue swept inside to stroke. It was rough and fast and just what she needed. She was bombarded from every direction. The taste and feel of him as he flattened her to the wall with his body, the ache in her breasts as they pressed against his chest. Through his open coat and clothes, her suit, she felt him and she liked it. The steely strength and heat, the rock-hard arousal she wanted to rub against.

All from a kiss? One that used teeth and tongue and created too much need, whip-fast pleasure that made her want to forget everything else. Her father and Garret and the ring she knew would be beautiful.

Lost, wanting to be taken wherever this led, wanting to *feel* one last time before having to face the numbness of regular, everyday life, she kissed him back, seeking, finding a white-hot passion guaranteed to send her soaring. But at what cost?

The thought brought painful clarity, instantaneous regret. The raw wound inside her opened up as though split by a bolt of lightning. She jerked out of Tobias's arms and slid sideways along the wall, watching as comprehension dawned on his face.

What had she done? Not only to herself but to Tobias? He was Garret's best *friend*. And Garret— *Oh, Garret.*

Glaring at her, Tobias spat out a curse so full of disgust with her and the situation she'd created, the boundary they'd crossed, she flinched and closed her eyes, didn't open them again until she heard him slam into the stairwell.

Her hand over her mouth, she leaned against the wall, rubbing to remove the feel of him, but only managing to taste him more. *Stupid* was messing up a good thing, kissing her boyfriend's best friend.

What goes on in that soft little head of yours, Jocelyn? Sometimes I think you're either too smart for your own good or too stupid to live.

Stupid was proving her father right.

TOBY BURST out of the gallery via the back door. *Where all the bottom feeders come and go in Debutante World.*

He shook his head and kept going, sludging through the deep snow and not giving a damn about what it did to his best suit.

Garret was going to kill him. It wasn't anything less than Toby deserved after what had just happened, but he'd already lost his job. He didn't want to lose his best bud in the same day. *Then why did you kiss her back?*

He growled out a curse and climbed into his Jeep, but after starting it he sat there a long moment, too angry to drive, too dangerous behind the wheel until he calmed down.

Jocelyn's passionate speech about not being a china doll had nearly destroyed what was left of his restraint, but the hold he'd managed to maintain unraveled the moment she'd crushed her lips to his. It was the desperation in her that had gotten to him. The way she'd gripped him, clung to him, the little moans in her throat because it had felt so right.

He hit his palm against the steering wheel. Screwed. He. Was. *Screwed.* No job. No best friend once Jocelyn went running to Garret, desperate to save her own neck in case he told Garret that she'd made the first move. Did it matter who'd crossed the line when all he'd wanted to do was have her up against the wall?

Maybe it *was* a good time to contact that head-hunter, he thought, shoving the vehicle into gear. A job in Siberia might come in handy right now.

CHAPTER FIFTEEN

"I JUST WANTED to let you know I received the flowers. They're beautiful, Garret. Thank you."

A slow smile spread across his face at the sound of Joss's voice on the other end of the line. "I'm glad you like them. Joss, about today—"

"I'm *sorry.* Garret, I had no right to go off on you like that and—I love you. You know that, right?"

"I love you, too." He frowned at her tone, the thready, anxious pitch so unlike her. "Is something wrong?" He thought he heard a sniffle. "Joss?"

"Garret, I—I need to tell you something."

"What?" He listened carefully, but didn't hear anything that sounded like she was crying. It was winter, a sniffle could mean anything.

"I—I…" She inhaled shakily. "I'm going to Montana."

"What? Why? When?"

"Tomorrow morning. Early. An artist I want to showcase isn't returning my messages, so I've decided to fly out and talk to him in person."

"What about the gallery? Won't this throw you even more behind schedule?"

"A little."

"It's only one guy. Can't you find someone else to display?"

"No. I want this artwork. And things will move more quickly than I'd thought. It's just a matter of hiring some help. I'm sure I can get an art student to come work for a good recommendation. I won't be gone long. A few days at most."

"I'd love to see Montana. If I could get away, I'd come with you. We could spend a little quality time together."

"That would be nice, but I know now isn't a good time with the buyout, and this is a business trip. I won't be sightseeing."

"You'll be careful?"

"Yes. But I'd better go. I have a lot to get done before my flight in the morning.... Garret? I'm sorry about today. Really."

"We just had a spat, Joss. It's okay. When you get back, we'll go out to dinner and you can tell me all about your trip. We'll make a special date of it. Maybe go to Biltmore and spend the weekend."

"That sounds lovely. Good night, Garret. Don't work too hard while I'm gone, and remember I love you."

"I love you, too." Hanging up, Garret frowned

down at the phone and sighed. Joss had sounded tired and stressed and upset, so maybe taking off and getting out of town for a few days would do her some good. And in the meantime?

He glanced at his watch and groaned. It was late; he was dead tired; and he still had to drop by Gram's and check on Darcy. How much longer could he go on like this? He could feel the candle slowly burning out, but too many people depended on him and he couldn't let them down. Grabbing his briefcase, he headed out the door.

Exactly twelve minutes later he shoved his thoughts about his job aside and drank in the sight of Darcy's smiling face on the other side of the condo's threshold. The mountainous tension inside him eased. "I take it things are going well?"

Her smile widened, her brown eyes warm and sparkling with welcome. "She's fantastic as you well know. Garret, it seems all I ever do is thank you, but thank you. Again."

"You're very welcome." He waited for her to step back before entering the condo and closing the door, noting immediately that Darcy's suitcase was no longer in sight. "You've unpacked?"

"Are you kidding? The moment I agreed to stay, Rosetta wheeled my suitcase down the hall herself."

He chuckled, able to picture the scene. "I knew

she'd convince you." He looked around but neither saw nor heard Gram. "Where is she?"

"Taking a bath. She should be out soon." Darcy led the way to the living room and dropped onto the couch. "Have you had dinner? We made stew."

"I ate at my desk around six. I should've called but it's been one of those days. Are you tired? I could go and let you get some rest."

Darcy hugged a pillow to her side as though trying to disguise her stomach. The move was automatic and reeked of her being self-conscious around him, but he thought her beautiful in her pregnancy, not awkward or ungainly. He had to fight hard not to stare at her full breasts.

"Actually, Rosetta insisted I lie down this afternoon. I did it to humor her and wound up falling asleep for three hours."

"You're still recovering from your adventure. Spike must've needed more rest." He'd referred to the baby as Spike several times now, but for some reason it seemed to fit. Darcy's child would be feisty and independent—just like its mother.

"Maybe, but now I'm not sleepy at all. I've been sitting here playing solitaire." She raised an eyebrow and gave him a cheeky grin. "You're not a card player are you? Blackjack? Gin?"

A quick game until Gram emerged might be just the thing to help him relax before heading home. He needed something to take the edge off. "Black Jack."

She shuffled the cards with the expertise of a cardshark.

"I think I've been had."

A soft, sexy laugh was his answer.

"You can't do this. Jocelyn, have you lost your mind? You leave now and that woman will have Garret to herself. You'll be history."

Jocelyn stalked into her bathroom carrying the bag she'd retrieved from the closet and began packing her toiletries. Of all times for her father to feel the need to talk to her about Garret, why did it have to be now when she already felt so bad? "Daddy, please. We're fine. For pity's sake, she's *pregnant.*"

"People are talking."

"Then let them talk! You know as well as I do that if the baby were his, he'd have married her already."

"You should never have started that monstrosity. It's ruining your relationship with Garret. Your future!"

That *monstrosity* would be her saving grace one day, that much she knew. "Oh? What am I supposed to do while Garret works eighty hour weeks? Sit home and twiddle my thumbs?"

"Your mother gave up this nonsense when she married me."

Which is why her mother was downstairs on her

third glass of wine instead of in a studio creating. "Thank God Garret would never ask me to do that." Her cell phone rang, and she left the bag to hurry and dig it out of her purse.

"Let it ring."

"I'm waiting on a business call."

"At this hour?"

"Overseas," she muttered, uncaring who it was so long as it ended the conversation. "Hello?"

"Garret hasn't come after me and tried to kill me. You didn't tell him?"

Tobias. Oh, what next? "Yes, I have been waiting on your call. Please hold for a moment." She pressed the phone to her chest. "I have to take this."

Her father glared at her. "You'll do well to remember what I said, Jocelyn." He stalked out of her bedroom and slammed the door behind him.

Joss took a deep breath and reluctantly raised the phone back to her ear. "What do you want?"

Toby made a tsking sound. "Using me to get rid of Daddy? Whatever should I think?"

"Tobias—"

"You didn't tell Garret."

What could she have said? *Oh, Garret, of course we're getting married when or if you ever ask, but I kissed your best friend and that's okay, right?*

"No, I didn't say anything. And I'm sorry. I don't know what came over me. But it's done and it won't happen again. I was upset and—You must think I'm a horrible person, but I regret it and I *am* sorry."

"I'm not."

"You don't mean that. I'd appreciate it if you'd keep the matter between us, too. Garret doesn't need to know. It would only hurt him."

Silence. What was he thinking? Would he tell Garret anyway? Had he already? No, no, Garret would've been upset when she'd talked to him.

"Have you seen him? Has he kissed you since then?"

She'd thought about going to say goodbye to Garret in person but couldn't bring herself to do it. She needed space, time to process and deal with whatever had made her behave the way she had.

It won't happen again. No, it wouldn't. Passion couldn't be trusted, couldn't be controlled, and she valued control. Needed it. This afternoon was an example of that and why it was all wrong. She'd allowed her body to lead her astray once, how could she have succumbed again?

No, she wanted a normal life with a normal man, not one who made her do things she'd *never* otherwise consider.

"Answer me, Jocelyn. Have you seen him? Did he kiss you?"

"That's none of your business. Good—"

"Don't hang up, we need to talk about this."

"No, we don't. What is there to say? I'm sorry. It shouldn't have happened. It was a *horrible mistake.*"

"Then why didn't it feel like one?"

She couldn't answer that, not even privately to herself. If she did, she feared her entire life would unravel. "It never happened. Do you hear me? It never happened and it will never happen again. Please, Tobias, don't tell Garret. I want to marry him. I love him. Don't ruin our future together because of one moment of insanity."

"Was it—"

"I have to go. Goodbye, Tobias."

CHAPTER SIXTEEN

GARRET WHISTLED as he waited outside Gram's condo. The sun was setting outside, and for the first time in ages he'd exited the hospital when it was technically still daylight.

The door opened and even though he hadn't been to The Village to visit much in at least two years, Gram didn't seem surprised to see him for the fourth night in a row. He and Darcy had played cards, watched movies, talked about everything from UFC Fighting to deep-sea fishing and helped with Bingo night downstairs. It was the most fun he'd had in years.

"Well, don't just stand there, come in," Gram ordered.

A burst of laughter filled the air and he frowned. *Nick?* Garret crossed the threshold and sure enough there sat Nick and his son, Matt, with Darcy around a table full of food.

"Garret, you're just in time." Darcy's cheeks colored with a pretty blush. "Are you hungry?" She scooted back her chair to stand.

"No, dear, you sit. I'll get my grandson a plate and something to drink." Gram pulled out the chair opposite Nick on her way to the kitchen.

"Thanks, Gram." Garret nodded at Nick and turned his attention to his nephew. "Hey, Matt. Wow, look at you. You've grown two feet since I saw you last."

"You saw me at Christmas."

"Has it been that long?"

Matt grinned, his mouth missing a few teeth. "Dad says I'm the bottomless pit. Maybe that's why." A third-grader, Matt had taken a growing spell this past year and no longer looked like a little kid. He was tall for his age, lanky, growing into that awkward stage. Something all the boys in the family had suffered through.

He felt bad that Matt was growing up and none of them were getting to see it happen.

Garret seated himself and smiled at Darcy. "What's going on here?"

Darcy fussed with her napkin and unleashed one of her amazing smiles on Nick. "Your brother came by so we could celebrate our deal. He finished the estimate on the repairs and he's going to let me work off the cost at the gym. I'm his temporary massage therapist. Isn't that sweet of him?"

Nick shrugged like it wasn't a big deal. "I've been looking for someone and already had a massage table on order. This benefits us both."

Darcy turned her cocoa eyes back to Garret, excitement etched on her features, and his gut pinched in response. How could he ever have thought she wasn't beautiful?

"It's more than that. He's already talked to some of his members and lined up clients for me. I start Saturday."

Jerking into the present, he frowned. "Are you sure you're up for it?"

"I'm fine."

"I'll keep an eye on her," Nick promised. "She won't overdo it." He settled back in his chair and palmed his coffee cup, raising it to his lips to drink.

Garret knew he ought to be reassured by Nick's words, but was Nick helping Darcy to be nice—or because he was interested in her? And what if he *was?*

Garret rubbed his chin. The fatigue was getting to him. He hadn't slept more than a few hours each night since Darcy left. Maybe he should get a massage? Help her out financially? Remembering what happened last time, he quickly decided against it.

"Something wrong?" Nick asked.

Gram returned from the kitchen. "Matt, be a dear and carry in the dessert for us?"

"Yes, ma'am." The kid took off like a shot, eager to please. "Gram, you made my favorite!" Matt returned with a broad smile on his face, the heaping plate of chocolate chip cookies balanced precariously in his hands. "Can I take some and go watch cartoons since I already ate?"

"Yes, sweetheart. Just take a napkin and try not to spill, all right?"

"Yes, ma'am."

"I didn't expect to see you tonight, Garret. Joss hasn't made it home yet?"

He glanced at Darcy, noticed her gaze focused on her plate. "She'll be back tomorrow afternoon. Her persistence paid off. She handpicked some pieces and is bringing them with her."

There was a lull in the conversation and he glanced at Nick, found his brother's gaze on Darcy. Not good. With her belly hidden and the light shining through the window behind her, it was all too easy to find Darcy attractive. Any man would.

A jab of anger slid through him that smacked of jealousy. Nick and Darcy might understand each other because of the similarities in their lives, but Nick needed to keep his distance. She didn't need the complication of a temporary romance at the moment.

Of course, she was strong enough to take care of herself—she'd proven it time and again. So why was he worried about Nick? Why was he feeling so protective?

Over the next half hour he didn't come up with any answers. The talk continued and eventually made its way down memory lane, thanks to Darcy asking questions about what it was like growing up in a large family. He and Nick talked about the good times they'd had, keeping Darcy and Gram laughing while they told on themselves and relived the pranks they'd pulled. It took him a while to realize Darcy worded her questions so that he and Nick remembered the good times and not the arguments over school and the split Nick had made from the family.

"I need more coffee. I'll be right back." Gram excused herself, wiping tears of laughter from her eyes, but Garret saw her linger at the door and smile in Darcy's direction. The sight was a punch to his gut. Gram loved Joss, but he'd never once seen her look at Joss that way.

"So, Darcy, you all settled in?" Nick asked.

"Yes, I am. The spare bedroom is beautiful, and Rosetta's—"

"Somebody's cell phone is ringing!" Matt called from the other room.

Darcy gasped. "That must be my mom. Excuse me."

And that's when he knew he was in deep.

He was protective because after knowing her only a week, he hated the thought of her leaving.

IN THE BEDROOM Darcy grabbed the phone from the bedside table where it charged. "Hello?"

"Darcy? Baby, are you all right?"

Relief poured through her. "I'm fine now. Mom, where have you been? I've left messages every day."

"Well—" her mother laughed "—I didn't check them because we took a little vacation to Vegas."

We? She knew that tone. "Mom, I told you I was on my way. Please tell me you didn't—"

"Things happen fast around here. You know that."

"What things? Mom, what did you do?"

"I got married! Now, I know what you're thinkin', but he's a good man, Darcy. It's sudden, but I think he's got sticking power."

For how long? Before she could ask, she heard the distinct sound of her mother lighting up a cigarette. "I thought you quit."

"I did, but Arnie smokes, too, and I got started back. You know how it is."

"Mom, you know how I was with my allergies as a kid. It won't be good for the baby to be around smoke." A long pause sounded on the other end and with every second that went by, Darcy's dread grew. "Mom? You are still planning on helping me with the baby, aren't you?"

"Darcy, I was, honest. But I've been thinking about that a lot and I've decided you can't expect me to pitch in and take care of your problems."

Take care of her *problems?* "Mom, please. Don't do this. I only asked you to help until I could get back on my feet. Until I can find a job and an apartment. Day care I can trust. I make good money, it won't take long."

"You don't know that. We're not the big city here and it could take a while before you find something. Which made me think— Darcy, you're plenty old enough to handle things on your own."

"But right after the baby is born—"

"You'll do fine. Why, women used to have babies and go out into the fields to work. Some still do. Having a baby is nothing these days. I'm sorry, honey, but I've changed my mind."

"Mom, you said you would help me. You promised. I packed up and *moved*."

"Don't take that tone with me. Beggars are beggars and I've got enough stacked against me without you being here with a squalling brat and— Look, don't take this personal and get all upset like you always do, but I never told Arnie I had a daughter, much less that I'm going to be a *grand*-mother, and I'm certainly not going to tell him now that we're married."

Hurt cut deep. She'd always known her mother lacked maternal warmth and depth, but to pretend she didn't even *exist?*

"Arnie's a bit younger than me, but we get along fine. If you come home and move in, well, I don't think a new marriage should have that much stress."

A bit younger? "How old is he?"

"Now, Darcy—"

"How old, Mom?"

"Twenty-eight."

Her mouth dropped. "He's only three years older than me?"

"Now do you understand? You'll do fine on your own, you always have. See if the daddy'll pay you to keep the baby away from him. Maybe then you could hire a nurse or something if you need one right after."

Keep the baby away. Like her mother wanted her to *stay away.* "I don't want Stephen's money. I never did."

Her mother snorted. "If you had his money now, you wouldn't be in this mess, would you? Darcy, I don't want to fight. As soon as you get your car fixed, you let me know where you wind up. Send me a picture of the baby at work. Not at home, okay? Don't forget and mess this up for me. I've got a good thing this time. Oh, I hear Arnie pulling in. Don't be mad, baby. Mama loves you."

The phone clicked in her ear. Darcy flipped the cell phone closed and tossed it aside. Then grabbed the doll she'd set on the bedside table and flung it to the floor. Glaring at its twisted appearance, she laid gentle hands on her stomach. "Mama loves you," she whispered, hugging her baby. A knot formed in her throat, too big to wish away.

Using her toe, she rolled the doll over so she could see its face, remembering when she thought her mother had given her the doll to show her how much she loved her. What a joke. Her mother didn't feel anything for her. "Don't worry. I'll protect you and take care of you, hold you when you're scared and always help you because that's what mommies are supposed to do. Don't be scared, because we're going to be all right. I'm not her. I'm not *her.*"

GARRET AVOIDED his brother's suspicious expression after Darcy left the room. He'd seen a lot of pregnant women come and go at the hospital, but Darcy was surprisingly graceful, and his gaze had lingered on her a lot longer than it should've. If not for the mound of her stomach, she wouldn't even look pregnant. And if she wasn't? Would that make anything easier?

"The baby yours?"

His attention snapped to Nick. "No."

"You sure?" Nick lowered his voice. "Because the way you're looking at her makes it seem like a possibility."

Garret clenched his jaw. It was one thing to have doubts about Joss and their relationship, but tossing Darcy—and her unborn child—into the mix was just insane. "I feel bad for her. She's going through a hard time right now, and needs a friend."

"That may be, but you weren't looking at her like she's a friend."

Garret shifted in his chair. "You're seeing things. She's pregnant, or didn't you notice?"

"She's still a pretty woman. Not to mention smart and funny." Nick smirked. "And there are ways around a pregnant belly."

The comment sent images through his head and his body reacted in an instant. He realized then and there the baby wasn't a problem for him. What kind of man held an innocent baby at fault for his or her conception? Darcy would've stuck by the baby's dad if he'd been man enough to take on the responsibility.

"What are we talking about now?" Gram asked as she returned from the kitchen, coffeepot in hand. "Where's Darcy?"

"She got a call on her cell. She thought it might be her mother," Nick informed her.

"Oh, I hope so. The poor dear. She's tried all week to act like she wasn't worried, but I could tell she was. It's obvious she doesn't have the family support the two of you grew up with." She shook her head. "The ones who have it always seem to take it for granted."

Nick scowled at the gentle reprimand and stared at the table, a muscle ticking in his jaw.

Garret grabbed a cookie from the plate and stood, his body well under control thanks to Gram's appearance. "I'm going to go spend some time with Matt, then check on Darcy."

In the living room Matt had zoned out in front of the television watching *SpongeBob SquarePants*. Glancing over his shoulder to make sure Nick and Gram weren't behind him, he gave Matt the cookie, then continued on down the hall toward the bedrooms. The door across from Gram's was open, a three-inch crack allowing him to hear Darcy's choked sobs.

His heart thudded in his chest as he approached. "Darcy?"

She snapped to attention and wiped her face with trembling hands. He crossed the room, stepping over an expensive-looking doll dressed in Victorian-era garb and sporting a head full of curls similar to Darcy's. He shoved the cell phone aside to sit on the bed beside her, pulling her against his chest and ignoring her stiff posture.

"Shh." He pressed a kiss to her hair, rubbed his hands up and down her back. "Whatever it is, it'll be fine. Remember what Dr. Clyde said. You don't want to upset Spike, right?"

A muffled noise escaped her—a laugh?—before she buried her face deeper. The scent of her hair reminded him of orange groves and flowers, the feel of it soft in his hands. "What happened? Tell me, sweetheart." Her voice emerged muffled against his chest and he couldn't make out her words. "What?"

"She got married. To husband number *f-four*. She was in Vegas and that's why she d-didn't call me back." Her fingers gripped his shirt, the ragged sound of her voice tearing at his insides. "She *promised* me. She said she'd help with the baby and let me stay with her while I got on my feet. She promised."

He cursed the woman who'd treat her daughter this way. Darcy was on her own? Completely? What kind of person did that? What kind of mother?

"He doesn't even know we exist. She didn't tell him because she doesn't want us. Doesn't want me. She never did."

Biting back a curse, he pressed a kiss to her temple and cradled her closer, Gram's comment about family support repeating in his head. "Darcy—"

"It was stupid of me."

"What was, sweetheart?"

"Believing in her. I knew better. I *know* better. All my life she's tossed me aside any time a man came around. Why did I think she'd put us first now? Why did I think I could depend on her?"

Because she saw the good in people, not the bad. That insight into Darcy's personality came easily. She'd had a rough childhood from the sound of it, but Darcy still believed in the good. He gently wiped away the tears. "You'll be okay. You're not alone,

Darcy." Her gaze shifted to the doll lying on the floor and he wondered at the connection. He bent and picked it up. "Who's this?"

Darcy glared at the doll but made no move to take her from him. "Miss Potts. My mom gave her to me when I was little."

"Looks like you've taken good care of her." Whether she'd thrown the fragile, expensive-looking doll or it fell off the bed, it was no worse for wear. Darcy on the other hand…

"Now you know why I didn't say much when we talked about family. My family isn't like yours."

Darcy's lashes were spiky, her nose red, but she was beautiful, her eyes liquid pools of glazed brown. Her full mouth turned down at the corners, trembling. He wanted to press a kiss there to still them, wanted to make her smile. Do something to ease the pain she was feeling.

"She gave me the doll for my birthday." A rough laugh escaped her chest, thick and throaty. "We didn't have a lot of money and I'd begged for Miss Potts forever. Mom always said no."

He didn't like the tone she used. "What happened?"

"I came home from school and let myself into the house. But hours passed and she didn't come home. Not until my birthday the next day. Then there she was, all smiles and apologies. She admitted she'd forgotten to call someone to come watch me because she was…having too much fun partying with a guy. I wouldn't have wanted her to stop having a good time, would I?"

Dear God. How could someone be so reckless? So uncaring about their own flesh and blood? "How old were you?"

"Eight." A bitter smile flashed. "A self-sufficient eight. There was food in the house. Cereal and juice. I didn't starve and I was okay, but—I was alone. My mom…she had a lot of boyfriends. She made it easy for them. Anyway, I was afraid if they knew I was there alone, if I left the lights on… I kept a flashlight on under the blankets. Then there she was, carrying the stupid doll like it made up for what she'd done. She said it was to keep me company next time because obviously I was a big girl and didn't need to be watched."

He rested his chin on her head, holding her close because he couldn't make himself let go. "She didn't know what a treasure she had."

Darcy inhaled raggedly. "*I'm* the gatekeeper in my family, Garret. The one who always took care of her when the guys dumped her and moved on. She said it was my fault because they didn't want another man's kid."

"Not all men are like that." He wasn't.

"I knew I had to get out of there. If I didn't get away from her I'd never be my own person. I couldn't deal with her life and have the one I wanted for myself. It was hard to break ties, but I did it. I went to school, moved wherever the job paid best. Then I found out I was pregnant and I didn't want my baby to be completely alone. I thought my mom had changed. She said she had. It just makes me so angry." Her hand fisted in his shirt. "I *believed* her."

"You wanted your baby to know its grandmother. You left the father because he didn't deserve you or Spike. Those are good traits, Darcy, not bad. You're fighting to do what's right, and no one can fault that."

She sniffled, a husky chuckle emerging from her throat. "Another pep talk. You need to charge for those. Oh, look at you." She plucked at his tear-soaked shirt. "I'm sorry for crying all over you. You poor guy, it's hard being my friend, isn't it?"

CHAPTER SEVENTEEN

"NOT AT ALL." Garret tucked a curl behind her ear. "I like being your friend."

"Thank you. Me, too." She blinked rapidly. "You're a good man, Garret."

"Sweetheart, I don't want to put more pressure on you, but what are you going to do now?"

She inhaled a shuddering breath. "I'm not sure, but I'll be fine. It's good that I have to do this on my own. I have to get used to being a single mom, and there's nothing like jumping in with both feet, right? As soon as my car is fixed I'll figure something out. We'll be fine, just the two of us."

He smoothed his hand over her hair. "I don't doubt you will, but it's okay to admit you need help sometimes, that you need someone to lean on. You've got that in me, okay?"

"Do you ever feel that way?"

Maybe it was the moment, maybe it was the way she looked at him. Whatever it was, he had to answer honestly. "Yeah, I do." He smoothed his thumb over her cheek, his gaze dropping to follow the movement. Her lips were parted, moist, and he found himself unable to look away, unable to stop the tide.

Garret lowered his head, hesitating a scant millimeter from her lips. Warnings clanged in his head, but he breathed her in, so close but not touching, not kissing. So close that with every breath, every tremble of her lips, he wanted more.

A small, muffled moan escaped her throat when he finally closed the distance and brushed her mouth with his, softly, barely a kiss at all. But his every muscle tensed at the touch, molten lava firing his veins until his whole body burned.

He sealed his lips over hers and suppressed a groan. Darcy tasted hot and sweet, like Gram's chocolate chip cookies and tears and woman. He filled his hands with her soft curly hair, tilted her head and deepened the caress, unable to stop, each nudge of their tongues a delicious slip and glide.

"I have to say goodbye to Darcy first!" Matt's running footsteps thundered down the hall.

Garret practically launched himself from the bed. Darcy gasped and covered her mouth with her fingertips and a scant second passed before Matt barreled into the bedroom.

"Darcy, we're leaving."

Darcy remained on the bed, her face blazing with color, but thankfully Matt didn't seem to notice—

or comment on Garret standing in the corner with a death grip on the dresser's rounded edge.

"Will I see you at the gym Saturday?"

"Of course." She cleared her throat. "Absolutely. I'll be there, just like your dad and I discussed."

Watching the interaction from the sidelines, Garret attempted to harness the explosion of desire and was startled when the boy threw himself at Darcy and gave her a hug. Matt was usually reserved and shy, not one for making contact. Had he ever hugged Joss?

"Will you play Alien Racers with me?"

Darcy nodded, returning the embrace. "I sure will, sweetie. You'd better practice, though, because I got really good playing it on my breaks at the hotel."

Matt released her with a grin. "You won't beat me."

"Matt?" Nick appeared in the doorway.

He hadn't heard his brother walk down the hall or else he'd have headed Nick off. One look at Darcy's face and his brother would know.

Garret watched, the knot in his gut growing, as Nick took in the scene. Darcy on the bed, a fiery blush remaining on her cheeks, and unable to make eye contact, Garret standing as far away from Darcy as possible, as if—

They were guilty of something.

He met Nick's gaze briefly and knew that while Nick was curious about whatever was going on—

something Garret would like to know himself—his brother was the last one in the family who'd judge.

"Matt, come on, we've got to go. Darcy, I'll see you Saturday."

"Um, yes. Thanks for getting my portable table out of the car and bringing it to me. I have three appointments here over the weekend."

Nick nodded. "You're on a roll. You'll earn the money in no time. I'll pick you up about twenty to ten."

Darcy smiled at Nick in thanks, and Garret's gut tightened in response. He didn't want her smiling at Nick. And he didn't have the right to want anything where she was concerned.

"Thank you. I appreciate it."

Garret ran a hand over his head and squeezed the muscles in his neck. Protective was sounding damn possessive.

"Matt?"

"I'm coming." The boy shuffled off with one last wave to Darcy.

Garret stared at his feet. The ability to speak and say whatever needed to be said, the gift he'd relied on his whole life, didn't appear. He had nothing but a truckload of guilt and self-recriminations. Emotions he couldn't begin to name. Joss deserved better than him kissing another woman. Wanting another woman. He'd always despised men who strung women along, used them, uncaring of their feelings. He wasn't like that. People expected more of him. He expected more of himself.

"It's okay, Garret."

He looked up to see Darcy watching him, her gaze much too astute.

"Believe me, I understand how complicated this is."

"I didn't mean to take advantage of your upset. That wasn't my intent."

A sad smile pulled at her lips. "I know. We're both stressed and feeling… I don't know. It's no big deal, just a kiss."

"You're sure? You're okay?"

Her chin raised, but her lashes lowered. "I'm fine."

She didn't look fine. She looked unhappy and dazed. And he felt like the lowest of the low because he had no right to make things worse. "I should go, too. Darcy, I'm sorry. That shouldn't have happened."

JOSS EMITTED a surprised shriek before clamping her hands over her mouth, staring in horror-filled shock at the sight that greeted her on the other side of her bedroom window. She'd tossed the drapes back to investigate a noise and there he was. Tobias glared at her, a hundred-eighty pounds of furious man. She glared right back. "What are you *doing?*"

"Open up."

She shook her head firmly back and forth.

"Do it or I'll go knock on the front door."

She opened the window a scant inch. "Go away. I don't want to talk to you." She tried to slam the window closed, but Tobias's hand shot out and kept that from happening. He raised the window higher, inserting one leg into her bedroom, then the other. "No, no. Get out. I said go away, not come in. I don't want to talk to you."

"Fine. I'll leave." Tobias headed toward her bedroom door.

"Stop! Wait!" She ran after him and flung herself in front of the door, glowering at him.

"Make up your mind, princess."

"Go out through the window."

"Not until we talk."

"I have nothing to say to you."

"Why did you take off? I've been through hell this week wondering what was going down with you."

"I—" she started to automatically say *I'm sorry* but refused to apologize again "—had a business trip."

"Uh-huh. You left because of what happened."

"Your ego is huge, you know that? I went to buy artwork."

"And to escape the fallout if I told Garret about what you did?"

"You wouldn't do that."

"What makes you so sure?"

She stared into his lion eyes and knew they both

felt the same in one aspect if nothing else. "You wouldn't hurt him that way. Just like I wouldn't."

"We kissed—"

"And I said I was sorry. Just *leave it be*."

"I can't. I can't, and do you want to know why?"

No.

"Your tongue was in my mouth and you kept inching your leg higher, like you wanted to wrap it around my waist." He eyed the paneled wood behind her. "Ever done it standing up?"

"Stop it."

"The idea getting to you? Join the club. I've thought of nothing else since that day."

She didn't comment. She wouldn't. He could talk all he wanted and when he was through, he'd leave. And if he so much as put a finger on her she'd scream.

With pleasure?

"How can you marry him knowing you want me?"

Her face burned. "It was a very *brief* moment in time. A mistake. And I'll marry him because I care for him and it's the right thing to do. This conversation isn't right. Nothing about this is *right*."

"You weren't thinking it was wrong when you kissed me."

"Would you stop saying that?" She slid sideways against the door and crossed the bedroom to get away from him but he followed her. "You're supposed to be his best friend. Where's your loyalty? Your honor toward Garret?"

"I guess I'm thinking that if you're kissing me, maybe this marriage isn't such a great idea. *There's* my loyalty. Maybe I'm doing my part to keep you both from making a mistake. He hasn't asked you, and you haven't been pressuring him to hurry up. That doesn't spell trouble to you? There's still time to fix this."

"Fix it? How could we possibly fix what we did?"

"By doing it again? If it was a fluke or—what did you call it? A mistake? Then we'll feel nothing and there's no reason for either one of us to be worried. Let's try it and see."

"That's ridiculous." She tried to put a wing chair between them, but Tobias snagged her arm and wouldn't let go. Still, he didn't attempt to follow through on his threat to kiss her again. "Let go." She yanked her arm free, knowing full well if he'd wanted to hold on to her, he could have.

"Is that what you want? Him? Take me out of the equation. If things were all right between the two of you, you wouldn't have kissed another guy. Admit it. Who's to say you're not going to go kissing someone else?"

"You know I'm not like that."

"How's that when you did it to me, his very best friend?" Tobias tilted his shaggy head to one side.

"That mean desire got the best of you?" He looked extremely pleased by the thought.

"It shouldn't have happened. I regret it."

Tobias crossed his arms over his chest, his gaze narrowed on her thoughtfully. "Are you sure you regret it? That kind of passion doesn't happen every day."

She struggled to focus, her hands fisting even though she'd never struck another living soul in her life. "That kind of passion leads nowhere and I won't be a part of it again." The moment the words were out of her mouth she knew she'd said too much.

"This is getting interesting. Again, huh? Who was he?"

"Leave. Now."

Once more he stopped her and kept her close. "Does Garret know about the guy or are you keeping him a secret, too?"

"It was a long time ago."

"He doesn't know, then."

"He knows I was with someone."

"What happened?"

"I fell in lust and thought it was love. End of story. Surprised?"

"That you could experience lust? No, you're a very passionate woman."

Garret didn't think so. She saw it in his eyes whenever they were together. Sometimes she'd been able to get into things and enjoy the closeness, but lately…

Tobias stepped forward, lifted his hand and smoothed his knuckles along her cheek. "Jocelyn? What are you afraid of? Are you afraid of feeling too much? Is that it?"

"I'm *not* discussing this with you."

"Why not? Obviously you can't discuss it with Garret. Tell me."

"Fine. You want to know? I don't trust blazing, gotta-have-you-now desire. It's pure lust and it means next to nothing. I had that and I got burned."

"How?"

"He used me for money and when I couldn't give him any more to fund his art, he left. End of story. Are you happy now?"

A muscle ticked in his jaw. "So you're going to marry Garret because he *doesn't* make you burn?"

Why wouldn't he just shut up?

"I don't like the thought of you getting hurt because some ass used you and abused you. But I'm not him. I don't want your money, and I'm man enough to know something special when I see it. When I *feel* it. That kiss—"

"Was nothing. Just like I had before. What about the guilt and pain we'd feel? What about decency? What about Garret?"

"He's a man, not a little boy. The question is,

are you a woman or a little girl playing at being an adult? You only get one life, Jocelyn. You either live it or you drag yourself through it. I love Garret like a brother, but the two of you are not married. You're not even engaged. You have time to fix the mistake by ending this before it gets worse."

"You don't care that it would hurt him? Humiliate him? We've been together three *years*."

"Garret is going to hurt a lot worse when you finally realize second best isn't good enough. You think he won't feel that? Living with you every day? Men aren't as stupid as women think."

"Garret and I are fine."

"Keep lyin' to yourself, honey. But we both know differently, don't we?" His yellow-gold eyes were hooded, darkened by thoughts she could easily read. Why? Why did she feel this way toward Garret's friend? Toward *anyone* else? Garret had supported her dreams, been faithful and kind. Loyal. He deserved more than to have her behaving like this or having this discussion at all.

She could be happy with Garret. Would be happier if Tobias— What? Stayed away? So now she was going to turn into her father? "Sex isn't everything. The grass isn't always greener on the other side. There are a million and one reasons why we'd never work. Even if Garret and I split up, I wouldn't be comfortable dating his best friend. What kind of woman does that?" Her father would never approve.

You're nearly thirty years old; why do you need Daddy's approval?

"Garret and I make a wonderful couple. We're friends. We complement each other very well, what with our backgrounds and—" She broke off abruptly, not wanting to hurt Tobias but managing to anyway. She saw it in his eyes, the sudden stillness in him.

"Your backgrounds and upbringing in Beauty's elite?" His face turned into a mask of disdain. "I'm just the maid's son, is that it? Someone to play around with and tease when you're bored but not to be taken seriously?"

"Tobias, please, I didn't mean it like that. I meant—"

"I know which damn fork to use, Jocelyn." He smirked. "One of the perks of being the housekeeper's son is that you pick up on things like that."

"I'm sorry. I didn't mean to insult you."

Tobias swung his leg over the sill, pausing long enough to say, "You didn't. You insult yourself by not seeing what you could have if you were brave enough to stand up to your old man and Garret instead of floating along afraid of your own shadow."

He was gone in a flash. One minute he sat on the edge of the sill and the next she saw him slip over the side of the roof out of sight.

Her shoulders sagged. Shaken, she closed the window and locked it. Pulled the drapes so that her room looked the same as it had before he'd arrived. He was crazy. Everything Tobias had said was just crazy. *Garret* was her future.

Not his best friend.

CHAPTER EIGHTEEN

Dr. Clyde frowned at Darcy after looking over the contents of the file folder in her hand. "Darcy, I'd hoped things would change since I saw you last, but I'm afraid I'm going to have to get strict here and put my foot down. You are not to travel alone, much less finish this move by yourself." The woman pulled off her reading glasses and gave Darcy a regretful stare. "Your blood pressure is still up and those cramps we talked about probably are some strong Braxton-Hicks contractions. But the fact they're not ending concerns me. I don't want you taking off and going anywhere without a traveling companion."

Darcy tried to unglue her tongue from the roof of her mouth. "But—my blood pressure is probably just up because of stress." *And Garret's kiss.* She'd had the hardest time forcing herself back into the kitchen to help Rosetta clean up and she'd caught the older woman looking at her suspiciously more than once. After the dishes were done, she'd claimed exhaustion and locked herself in her room, somehow managing to avoid the subject of her mother's call. Thank God the woman didn't pry. "I'm fine," she told the doctor. "I feel a lot better since I've rested."

"Stress is another thing you must get under control. Even with all that you're facing. If you don't, your problems are going to get worse. Stress manifests in health issues, and we can't have that with this baby. Surely you have someone who can fly down and drive you home to Indiana?"

"There's only me and my mom, but she can't come. Actually, I'm not sure I'm going to move to Indiana now." She had the week until her car was repaired to figure it out. Not much time in the scheme of things. Was she seriously thinking of driving off on her own after what Dr. Clyde said? What about being responsible?

"You aren't going to stay with her?"

Feeling the doctor's censure, she shook her head, unwilling to part with more humiliating details. She could only imagine what the doctor thought of her situation. For all intents and purposes, she was homeless. Dr. Clyde wouldn't report her or believe her unable to take care of her baby, would she?

"Darcy, look at me." The doctor waited for her to

obey. "Your baby doesn't need a lot of expensive toys or gadgets. But it does need you to be as healthy as possible. You need to establish roots and *quickly*. Getting settled and having plans for the future should bring your blood pressure down. I'm going to be blunt and give you advice you probably don't want to hear. I think you need to rent a place in Beauty and stay until after the baby arrives. I don't think we need to put you on Brethine yet, but if the low-grade cramping turns into more, I want you here immediately." She patted her hand. "I don't want you to be alone and I hope you feel you can trust me to help you through this. I'll do as much as I can for you to make sure you and your baby are okay."

"Thank you." Darcy struggled to keep her emotions under control. The past twenty-four hours seemed surreal. Her mother, Garret and his horror over the kiss. This. Dr. Clyde's advice was sound. She had to find her own place. No way could she stay with Rosetta until the baby was born. And Garret? Would he feel strange visiting her now? Probably so if his reaction last night was anything to go by. But her car wasn't ready yet, and she couldn't leave or move without it.

"We'll need to set up weekly appointments from here on out, but come before then if you experience any changes or problems. Go back to where you're staying until your car is repaired, prop your feet up.

Check out the apartment rentals in the paper, and get some rest. Doctor's orders." She ripped off the diagnosis sheet and handed it to Darcy. "I'll see you in a week."

Outside the office, Darcy put one foot in front of the other. What now? Stuck on that highway that night, she'd prayed for a miracle and received a series of disasters instead. The knot in her stomach grew to monstrous proportions and she ducked into the ladies' room. The panic grew larger, more strangling. She had limited funds. Maybe Nick would let her stay in the massage room at the gym until she got some money together. Surely there was a locker room. An office? Sleeping on a couch would be fine. The gym had showers.

Darcy left the restroom and rode the elevator, ignoring the curious looks from the smocked nurses and orderlies because no matter how hard she tried she couldn't stop biting her lips and twisting her fingers into pretzels. What was she going to *do?* Why had she kissed Garret? If they hadn't shared that kiss everything would be normal between them now. She'd feel comfortable staying at Rosetta's until she found an apartment, her conscience clear. But not now.

Darcy left the elevator and turned the corner only to hesitate beside the foliage of a ten-foot ficus tree, her gaze locking on Ethan and Garret standing about four feet away arguing, if the expressions on their faces were anything to go by. Stepping closer but remaining behind the tree, she listened.

"Darcy is nice, okay? She's *great,* but do you know how long I've waited for the chief of surgery to retire? I planned to toss my hat into the ring officially, but when I went in to talk to Harry, I couldn't get a word in because Harry was on a rampage about you and how you've betrayed Joss by having an *affair* this week while she was gone."

Garret ran a hand over his face. "Didn't you explain?"

"I didn't get the *chance.* Garret, you've gotta fix this and do it quickly. Propose to Joss as planned, put the ring on her finger and make it official so Harry will calm down."

Darcy caught her breath. *Propose? As planned?* They were *that* involved? But Garret had kissed *her* and— *It meant nothing.* He'd regretted kissing her, said he was sorry. She was the one who'd thought that maybe it wasn't such a mistake. That friends could become more.

"When I propose to Joss, it won't be because Darcy needed a place to stay and Harry's using it to his advantage to force my hand."

When, not *if.* The ache in her back increased and Darcy lifted her hand to rub it. The movement drew

Garret's attention and she smothered a groan, but managed a shaky smile. "Good morning."

Ethan swung to face her. "How long were you standing there?" His expression softened into one of doctorlike compassion. "You weren't meant to hear that, Darcy. This isn't your fault."

"Don't. I'm glad I know what's going on. And I'm sorry for causing you both trouble."

"You're no trouble. Everything is fine," Garret insisted.

"Yeah, once Garret explains the situation to his boss, it will all blow over. It's the old-fashioned mind-set around here, that's all."

"It might be old-fashioned, but I guarantee your family isn't any happier about this than I am."

Darcy jumped at the sound of the deep, angry voice, and turned to face the man it belonged to. Garret's boss? He had three chins, a rounded stomach way bigger than hers and wore a brown suit, overcoat and brown hat with a two-inch band of black piping at the base of the brim. The man regarded her with an uncompromising stare, his gaze sweeping over her and lingering on her belly before shooting back to her face.

"Darcy, this is my boss, Mr. Pierson. Harry, Ms. Darcy Rhodes."

"I can't say that I'm happy to make your acquaintance."

"Harry—"

"I do not appreciate the situation you've forced upon Garret or this hospital."

"She didn't force anything." Garret glanced at her, his moss-green eyes soft with regret.

Harold released a loud *harrumph*. "You're a brilliant man, Garret. I'd never have guessed you'd fall for some money-hungry bed-hopper's tricks."

"That is enough. Harry, I know why you're upset, but you have no reason to be."

Ethan moved so that he stood beside her. "I agree. You're insulting Darcy and Garret both—not to mention Joss—by suggesting something more happened than us simply giving a stranded, *pregnant* woman a roof over her head in the midst of a natural disaster. What kind of image would it have set if two of the hospital's employees had turned their backs on her?"

"Lending a helping hand is one thing, but it did not have to involve her sleeping in the same house— or visiting her every night this past week."

She should've known people were gossiping about them. How could she have forgotten that about small towns? In Miami no one knew or cared what went on with the neighbors unless the police showed up. But Beauty was even smaller than her hometown in Indiana, and everyone had known *everything* happening with her mother there. Thank goodness the kiss hadn't taken place outside the condo door.

The argument continued. People—hospital employees and visitors alike—gawked as they walked by. The pain in her back caused the muscles on her sides to ache, and she rubbed her stomach in rhythmic motions when the latest cramp grew stronger.

No. No, she wasn't doing this again. It was stress. She had to calm down and the pains would go away. Everything would be fine as soon as she could get away from them all, even Rosetta. She needed to retrieve her things from the condo and find a cheap room somewhere and lick her wounds in private.

Desperate to sit down, she spotted a bench nearby and lowered herself to the seat, earning a frowning look of concern from Garret. "Just resting. I'm fine."

"You don't look fine," Ethan murmured. "You're having contractions again, aren't you?"

She moved her head calmly back and forth. She was not their problem, not anymore. "I'm fine." But maybe she should go back upstairs. Things were getting a little… intense.

"Of course she's fine," Harry added. "Don't think a little playacting on her part is going to change the subject, Garret. You owe me and my daughter an explanation and an apology. How dare you treat Jocelyn this way?"

His daughter? Mr. Pierson was Garret's boss *and* future father-in-law? A pain sharpened.

Oh, yeah, you definitely need to go upstairs. Darcy pushed herself to her feet, hating that she appeared so awkward and huge. Tears pricked her eyes, the norm these days. She wasn't the type to cry over problems. Why bother when it didn't make them go away? She was more of a plow-through-until-you-figure-it-out kind of person. That got results and kept her too busy for tears.

Darcy worked to keep the discomfort from showing on her face. *Okay.* As soon as she could walk, she'd go upstairs. Calmly. Without an audience.

"That's it. Don't move." Ethan jogged to the nearby information desk and grabbed the handles of a wheelchair.

She shook her head in denial, but Garret took hold of her hand and wrapped an impossibly strong arm around her shoulders, lending her support. Her face burned. "Garret, please. Let Ethan help me. I don't want you to get into any more trouble."

Ethan turned the wheelchair around and set the brakes.

"I can walk."

"You ride or I carry you," Garret murmured, the look in his eyes stating he'd do just that. And how would that appear to the gawkers watching this scene? Before she could take him to task on giving her orders and kissing her when he planned to *marry* someone else, she found herself in the chair.

Garret squatted down in front of her. He lowered the footrests and placed her feet on top, maintaining his hold longer than necessary. "I'm sorry, sweetheart. We'll talk later, okay?"

"What's there to talk about?" she asked pointedly. "I understand." But did she? Garret didn't seem like the type of guy to go around cheating on women.

"Garret, shut up and get out of the way." Ethan unlocked the brakes and got them moving.

"I'm not finished with either one of you." Harry followed them to the elevator. "I want answers and I want them *now*."

The elevator doors opened, but as the brothers wheeled her inside, Rosetta called Garret's name.

"Aww, great," Ethan murmured.

Darcy glanced up and saw Garret close his eyes as though summoning the depths of his patience— or in embarrassment. She'd bet the latter. The older woman stepped onto the elevator with them, Garret's boss following her.

"What on earth is going on here? You've got people talking about you throughout the hospital."

"How are you, Gram?" Ethan kissed the woman on the cheek. "You look beautiful."

"Good morning, Gram." Garret smiled, but it was a strained effort.

Ethan pushed a button and the elevator began its ascent.

Harry dipped his head in a respectful nod. "Just the person I need to talk to. Rosetta, I want to know how you could condone such behavior. Why would you allow Garret to bring his pregnant mistress into your home and—"

"Harold Pierson, you should be ashamed of yourself! Don't let me hear another word like that." Rosetta glared at Garret's boss, then dropped her gaze to look Darcy over, her eyes narrowing shrewdly. Swallowing, Darcy prayed for them all to go away. As though sensing her thoughts, Rosetta nodded and patted Darcy's shoulder. "Let me handle this and don't fret, dear. It's not good for the baby."

The elevator arrived on Dr. Clyde's floor and Ethan pushed her down the hall at a breakneck pace, the others hurrying behind them. To her horror, the entire group followed her inside. Everyone in the waiting room looked up from their magazines and books. On the other side of a plexiglass partition, Dr. Clyde spoke with one of her employees, but the moment she noticed the hospital president and the rest of them in her waiting room, she walked out of sight. A second later the door to the examination rooms opened.

"Bring her right back. Darcy, what happened?"

She shook her head mutely, unable to speak.

"Oh, I know that look. They're back, huh? Room three. Becky will get you hooked up to a monitor and we'll see what's happening here. The rest of you, please, wait in my office."

Rosetta rested her hand on Darcy's shoulder. "May I stay with you, dear?"

Darcy nodded even though she knew she should say no. Things were complicated enough and she needed to get used to being entirely on her own. Right now, however, Rosetta's friendship was too precious to pass up. Within moments a fetal monitor was in place, a blood pressure cuff on her arm.

"Even higher than before. Darcy, I know you were upset by what I told you earlier. I could tell, but—"

"Excuse me for interrupting, but what did you tell her?"

Rosetta looked at her expectantly, and somehow Darcy managed to repeat the doctor's warnings.

"Oh, Darcy. Child, don't you dare worry about a thing. Do you hear me? You can stay with me. I don't mind."

"Rosetta, we're not talking about a week or even *two*."

"She's right," Dr. Clyde interjected. "She'll need a place to stay until she's cleared to travel, which could be anywhere from two to six weeks after birth."

"And I'm fine with that," Rosetta stated firmly. "Darcy, you shouldn't be alone now. And since your mother isn't able to come get you, I'd be honored if you'd consider my home yours. I have plenty of room and you can't think of yourself as a bother when you'd be giving us old people a lot of excitement waiting on a baby to arrive. You're welcome to stay as long as you need."

Her nose tingled with yet more tears. Were these people for real? How could anyone—total strangers—be so generous?

"I'm afraid we have a more serious problem here. The contractions started too easily and could progress without medication and monitoring. It's feasible that you could go into labor if we let the contractions continue. Darcy, you've got a little less than five weeks until your due date, but we need every one of them."

"I have to take the medication, don't I?"

"It would be best," Dr. Clyde said with a nod.

"Will I be able to work? I have to pay for the repairs and rent." She turned toward Rosetta. "If I stay with you, I have to pay rent. I'm *not* a charity case."

Rosetta's features softened with a look similar to…pride? "I know that, dear."

Dr. Clyde set her file aside. "In an ideal world I'd insist you not work. But given the situation, I'm not opposed to it if doing so will make you feel better, and provided the medication is effective and you aren't contracting. But you need to rest between clients, and I insist on half your normal load. Understood?"

Darcy nodded, unable to take it all in. It should've been her mother standing here beside her, should've been her mother holding her hand in support. Offering to help, to take her home. Garret wouldn't like this. Not after what happened between them. And his boss.

My baby comes first. And it's not like I'll be kissing Garret again.

Darcy forced herself to lift her chin and stare directly into Rosetta's eyes. "Are you sure?"

"Without a doubt."

"Then I'll stay on the condition that I pay you rent and get to help around the house."

Rosetta beamed. "Done. You drive a hard bargain."

Darcy smiled weakly. They all knew she was getting the best of the deal.

CHAPTER NINETEEN

LATER THAT EVENING Garret sat back in his chair and tried to tell himself he wasn't responsible for how complicated his life had become. It didn't work.

Despite Gram's assurances that she had things under control and that nothing had happened between Garret and Darcy, Harry had made life hell. When the hospital president wasn't muttering about Darcy and public display, he'd wreaked havoc throughout the hospital, causing numerous problems. And why not? Harry knew Garret would be the one left to clean up the mess. Garret didn't doubt it was Harry's version of revenge and the man's way of keeping him so busy he wouldn't have time to see Darcy.

After months of negotiations with the union representative and coming within inches of signing a new contract with the nurses, Harry had blown everything by informing the union official that the nurses didn't *deserve* a raise. Harry and the rep had nearly come to blows, and Garret had spent the entire afternoon on the phone trying to repair the damage. He was sick of Harry's temper and holier-than-thou attitude. The man didn't have a clue how to relate to the hospital's many employees. Months of work down the drain and for what?

As they had throughout the day, his thoughts drifted to Darcy. That her latest scare came on the heels of their kiss had been on his mind all day, and he tossed the pen he held onto the desk in frustration. How was she? Did she think he'd kissed her because— Why *had* he kissed her? One minute he'd offered comfort, the next he couldn't think of anything but tasting her. Friends didn't do that.

The phone rang and he hesitated before picking it up. "Garret Tulane."

"Sounds like you and I had the same kind of day," Joss said. "I just wanted to let you know I'm home and that I talked to Daddy a few minutes ago. He was awfully fired up."

"Yeah." He sighed. "Joss—"

"Don't worry about me, Garret. Daddy's in a mood. You're such an honorable man. I trust you and I know you'd never deliberately hurt me. And I would never deliberately hurt you."

Tell her what happened. But it was only a kiss, and not deliberate, like she'd said. Why make the situation worse when it wouldn't happen again?

"Listen, I, um, called to cancel our date tonight.

I know we talked about going out to dinner, but I'm really tired and—"

"No."

"What?"

"Joss…I don't care what we do. I don't care if you sleep all evening, but I'd like to see you."

"Oh… How sweet. Okay, I think maybe I feel a second wind coming. I'm at home. Want to swing by here?"

"I'll be there in half an hour."

"Good. Now stop brooding. Daddy will calm down soon."

He wasn't so sure. At least not without a major concession on his part. Maybe he should ask Joss tonight? Get it out of the way?

There you go again. That's nice and romantic.

"How is Darcy?" Joss asked, matter-of-fact. "Daddy said she went into labor again."

He'd bet that wasn't all Harry had said. "From the stress."

"Poor thing. Be honest, was Daddy involved?"

He blamed himself for upsetting Darcy, but Harry certainly hadn't helped. "Some. Anyway, she's stuck in town until the baby's born now. Ordered not to travel. If she can handle it, she'll be able to work. Nick's hired her on at the gym."

"That's great."

It was. If he didn't think too much about Darcy

putting her hands on other men. *Why* the thought of that bothered him was a question he couldn't answer.

"Garret, if you want to check on Darcy, don't let Daddy's temper stop you. Go right ahead."

He cleared his throat. "That's very understanding of you."

"She's pregnant and alone in a strange town. I can't imagine being that way and having no one. It's…sad. I understand why you feel the need to watch out for her—you're the one who found her that night. Now, I've got to go make myself presentable before you get here. See you in a little bit." Murmuring goodbye, she hung up.

Garret set the receiver on the base, his thoughts focusing on what Joss had said about Darcy. He was concerned about her, worried. Responsible. Maybe *that* was the source of his interest in her?

He grabbed his briefcase from the floor behind his desk and started to fill it only to pause. Harry had come in that morning with nothing in his hands, gone home the same way. Right or wrong, Garret had been performing Harry's job in a lot of ways of late. Anger surfaced. Harry had no right to terrorize the hospital with his tantrums, and he needed to learn the consequences of his bullying.

Garret mentally quelled the rising tide of guilt and self-imposed responsibility, and determinedly returned the briefcase to the floor. Nodding to himself, he grabbed his keys and coat and headed toward the door, feeling very much like a kid playing hooky from school.

Maybe it was time to not be so ready to step in. Time to back off and let Harry appreciate him a little more. Time to make some changes.

FORTY-FIVE MINUTES LATER Garret sat across the table from Joss at his uncle's bar and grille and thought of all the reasons she was perfect for him. Joss could play the socialite when expected, be charming and poised. She could also laugh at herself on occasion, and she was a smart, astute business-woman. So why didn't he ask?

She looked up, her fork raised halfway to her lips. "Something wrong?"

"I'm proud of you. You've done an amazing job on the gallery." Her lashes lowered, but Garret thought he saw a flash of resentment.

"Thank you."

"What?"

Joss stared at him blankly. "Pardon?"

"Don't give me that. You're angry. Why?"

"It's nothing."

"Obviously it's something."

She lowered her fork to her plate and gave him a benevolent stare. "How do you know I've done an amazing job? You've barely set foot inside the gallery. I didn't say anything because I don't want to fight."

"I've been busy."

"I know."

"Your father's my boss and not an easy man to take."

"I know that, too. How about we talk about something else? Your mother said the cake recipe for Rosetta's birthday party is divine."

So that's what they were down to? Discussing cake recipes because they couldn't talk about *them?* "How about we go back to the gallery after we eat? It's after hours so the phones will be quiet, no deliverymen will show up. You can give me a private tour."

She hesitated for a long moment. "Now? Oh, well…I suppose I could. No, I will. That sounds like…fun."

"What sounds like fun?" Toby walked up to the table from behind Joss's left shoulder.

Garret sat back and grinned at him. "Where have you been? You haven't been to the gym all week."

Toby glanced at Joss and then back at him. "Jocelyn didn't tell you?"

"Tell me what?"

"Tobias, I thought—I wasn't sure if—"

"I'm job hunting."

"What?" Garret looked at Joss and saw her staring

at Toby, her expression hard to read. What was up with that? He focused on Toby. "What happened?"

"Same old thing. I got strung along like a mule with a carrot, but didn't get the partnership."

"Ah, Tobe, tough break."

"Yeah, well, while I look around I've been taking some time to kick back and sleep in. I've been going to the gym later in the day."

"That's an excuse. You're just afraid you're off your game and I can take you down. Admit it, your record is history."

Toby smiled at the teasing. "Bring it on."

A pause followed the words and Garret shifted on the booth's seat. "I'm surprised I haven't talked to you if you're on the hunt. How many times have you mentioned partnering up? Change your mind?"

Toby shoved his hand through his hair. "You've, uh, got your hands full right now. I know it can't happen so why ask? Looks like my takeout is ready. See you around. Jocelyn…enjoy dinner with your guy, here."

"Later." Garret watched Toby walk away and then glanced back at Joss to see her gaze following him, too. "I can't believe Wellington did it to him again. Toby's a great attorney."

"He'll find something."

He frowned at her tone. "Joss, is something going on?"

She flashed him a cool, measured smile. "Nothing unusual. I have a headache. After I arrived home today I got another lecture from Daddy. He says we don't spend enough time together and that our relationship is suffering."

"Do you feel that way?" Garret watched her closely, looking for clues to what she was thinking.

"I'm not complaining if that's what you're asking. *I've* canceled our dates, too, remember? I haven't been able to spare more than a few minutes for you these past few months, and I understand that things are the same way with you. It just makes me wonder—" She broke off and jabbed her fork into her food.

"Wonder what?"

Another shrug. The silence between them lengthened, the weight of the ring box burning a hole through his pocket. If he asked, they'd be able to spend more time together and the tension between them would ease…right?

Garret finished off the last of his steak and downed the soda, noticing for the first time that other than the few bites she'd taken at the beginning of the meal Joss had barely eaten.

As though sensing his perusal, her light blue eyes rose to meet his. Out of nowhere he pictured a warm, rich toffee-colored gaze.

"Garret, can I be honest?"

"Absolutely."

"I'm not feeling very well tonight. Can we postpone the tour and make it an early night?"

He wasn't expecting that, but reminded himself that timing was everything. She had tried to call off the date and he hadn't let her. This was no less than what he deserved for forcing her to come. Still he wanted to talk to her about how she felt, what she saw for the future. Kids, house. What did she dream of?

He pushed his plate out of the way and leaned his elbows on the table. "Are you sure nothing's wrong?"

Her gaze darted away from his. "I'm really tired and not hungry at all. I have a nasty headache and there's this ongoing list of things to do buzzing around in my mind. I feel like I need to go to sleep and start fresh tomorrow."

"I was kind of hoping we could talk. There's something important I'd like to ask you."

The fork slipped from her hand and clattered onto her plate before bouncing to the wood floor. "Sorry. I'm such a klutz. I'll go get a new one from one of the stations. Your uncle won't mind, will he?"

"You just said you weren't hungry. Use mine, I'm finished."

"I'm not hungry, but—"

He grabbed his fork from his plate and placed it on the edge of hers to use or not use as she liked. "Joss, listen, I'm sorry I haven't been around to help you with the gallery. I apologize for that. I hope you're not upset with me and just not saying anything. You can talk to me."

"Don't be silly. You're busy and you've got more important things to do than mess with my little gallery."

"Joss—"

"Daddy certainly wouldn't want you wasting your time there when you could be working at the hospital. Besides, you're not interested in art at all."

"It's just not my—"

"Not your thing. I know—" she pushed her plate away "—and it's fine. Garret, really, I'm not very good company tonight. I think it's best if we go. I think I'm coming down with a touch of the flu or something. You know what? You stay. Go have a drink at the bar. I'll call a cab."

"Joss, sit down. You look pale. Maybe you're jet-lagged. Give me a second to take care of the bill and I'll drive you home."

JOCELYN GAZED out the window as Garret drove her home. He'd asked if she needed more air, if she felt sick. If he'd done something to upset her. All of which she answered with a low no. All of which she should have answered with a yes. She needed more air because she couldn't breathe, felt sick because of what she'd done. Was furious at Garret for spending so much time at the hospital with her father instead of with her. Where were her guts? Her backbone? Why did she play the good little girl and pretend?

Turning her head, she watched as the streetlights played over Garret's face. He was gorgeous. Strong and tall and handsome. A man's man. A man she'd be thrilled to call her husband. But was Tobias right?

Garret pulled up to the house and stopped, shoving the vehicle into Park before he reached for the door handle.

"No," she said quickly, unable to stomach the pretense a moment longer. "Don't bother walking me to the door. I'm going straight to bed. Thank you for dinner."

He snagged her arm before she could let herself out. Watching her closely, Garret slowly tugged and she moved toward him willingly, hoping, praying, that while she'd been gone something had changed.

Garret brushed his lips gently over hers. "Feel better."

She nodded, hesitated, then wrapped an arm around his neck and kissed him again, the kiss too hard. Desperate. Awkward and totally different from the way she'd felt with Tobias. She pulled away with a murmured goodbye and rushed out of the Escalade.

"Joss?"

"Yes?"

"I love you."

She turned to shut the door, blinded by tears. "I love you, too."

CHAPTER TWENTY

DARCY STARED up at Garret and laughed. "Shut up! Are you serious?"

He winked at her. "No one suspected a thing."

She lifted the hammer up to him and watched as he nailed the closet supports into place. Darcy was fairly sure Rosetta's maintenance contract covered such things, but the woman had insisted Garret was a better hand at completing the chores. Darcy was glad to see him again. After the kiss and that scene at the hospital, she wasn't sure how he'd treat her. If he would even come to see her.

"What's next on the list?"

"The shelf above the washer. It wobbles, apparently."

He tested the support, made sure it wouldn't budge and climbed down, seemingly as at ease on the ladder as he was at his job. The power player had a domestic side. Who knew?

Garret put the hammer back into the tool chest, hesitating. "Darcy, about the other day—"

"We're good. Right, Spike?"

He chuckled, his eyes warm on hers. "I'm glad. You and Spike have enough on your hands without me adding more to the mix."

"Or hurting your girlfriend," she murmured softly, nixing the easygoing mood with four words.

Garret hesitated, his expression darkening with a mixture of regret and sadness. "Or that."

GARRET FROWNED and hung up the phone when he got Toby's voice mail again. He knew his friend was upset about Wellington and the loss of the partnership, but Toby had bills to pay. He had to get something going soon, and a week had come and gone since that night at the Old Coyote.

A knock sounded outside his door. Garret swiveled in the chair, hoping Toby had come to see him, but his mother stood there instead. "Hey, Mom, what's up?" He stood and walked over to give her a kiss.

"You tell me." His mother hugged him back and sent him a look he recognized well. "Garret, is everything all right?"

Sighing, Garret leaned his hips on his desk and scowled. "If everyone would mind their own business, it would be."

"Have you been out with Joss lately?"

He inhaled and sighed. "She picked up a cold in Montana. I've talked to her on the phone several times, but she's been taking it easy and puttering around the gallery. Why?"

"Garret—"

"It's not my baby."

"Well, of course it's not. I know Darcy would be wearing a wedding band if that was the case." She smoothed her carefully styled hair. "Sweetheart, I hate to sound old-fashioned, but appearances do matter and—"

"Harry said something to you."

The first time or two he'd seen Darcy since the kiss, her responses had been reserved, but then she soon warmed up and seemed to have forgiven him. Once he started noticing the ripe fullness of Darcy's breasts pressing against her top, the curve of her lips and the shape of her behind, the way she jumped up to help Gram every time she thought the older woman needed it, he left. *But you still noticed.*

His mother drew herself up to her full height. "He's concerned. And frankly, so am I."

"It's fine, Mom."

"Then why are you doing this?"

"Doing what? Darcy is literally stuck here in town until after the baby's born, and Gram's great, but don't you think it's a little heartless to drop Darcy there and not see her again?"

"So it's friendship? She's your friend?"

"I'd like to think so, yes."

Exhaling what appeared to be a sigh of relief, his mother said, "We want you to be happy, Garret." She palmed his face in her hands. "Marriage is supposed to be forever. No one would hold it against you if you need more time before you propose to Joss."

"Harry would disagree with that statement."

"Harry can disagree all he likes. I don't want you or Joss hurting over something that could've been prevented if it wasn't rushed."

"Me, neither. Thanks, Mom." He forced a smile. "Now, tell me how the plans are going for Gram's big birthday bash."

DARCY ACCEPTED the gift with a smile. "Thank you, Mrs. Colby. I don't know what to say."

The older woman beamed. "You don't have to say a word, honey. I'm glad to help. My grandbabies have more than enough. I thought you might be able to use a little, too, with your baby on the way."

"I can. I appreciate it." It had been that way all day. All of her clients had come bearing gifts, and she was overwhelmed by their generosity. As she set the gift aside and selected music for Mrs. Colby's session, she reminded herself this was a temporary situation. She wouldn't be staying here, best not get too attached to the people.

But they're so nice. Why not stay?

Moving close to the door, Darcy spotted the flyers

that had appeared that morning. Jocelyn Pierson's name was displayed in bold letters as the event contact for donations benefitting the children's ward at the hospital. Garret's hospital where he worked for Jocelyn's father in the position Garret's grandfather helped him get. Garret was too nice a guy to screw with his life.

She enjoyed the time she spent with him. Loved how he made her laugh and blush and feel like a woman instead of a beached whale. But she liked it too much. He was too handsome, too flirtatious, too kind. Too nice a guy for her to have to sit back and watch him marry another woman.

That's why you can't stay.

JOSS APPEARED in front of Garret during his workout, looking every inch Harry's daughter in her sleek suit and high heels. "Hey, feeling better?" he asked.

"Yes, I am. Thank you."

"What's wrong?"

"You tell me. I just got off the phone with Daddy." Her light blue eyes narrowed in concern. "I can't believe he had the gall to say what he did to your *mother.* I'm so embarrassed. He treats me like I'm a child, not a woman."

Maybe if Joss spoke up more, Harry wouldn't do that. Garret smiled, grim, almost wishing she *had* put Harry up to it. At least then it would mean she cared enough to fight for him. How juvenile was that? But her mood of late worried him, and he wouldn't mind a little better idea of where he stood. They were two adults, but the pressure to keep their families happy was intense. This was why guys didn't bring the girl home to meet the parents until he knew for sure what he wanted. "Mom was fine. We had a nice chat when she came to see me about it." He nodded toward her clothes. "You working out?"

"No. I had to take my car to Nick's. It's making a funny noise."

"You should've said something. I could've had a look at it."

"You're too busy, and Nick said it would take ten minutes. A fan belt or some such. I saw your car and thought I'd come to apologize. I don't know what's gotten into Daddy lately. He's so insistent that we make things permanent."

"I'm sorry, sweetheart. You don't need that pressure on top of getting ready for the opening."

"I'm okay. So why are you here now? I thought you always worked out in the morning?"

"I was hoping to run into Toby."

"Oh? Any particular reason why?"

"I think he's feeling pretty low about not getting the partnership. Thought I might try to cheer him up. Guess I'll track him down some other time. Want to grab some dinner? I'm almost done here."

She shook her head. "That sounds lovely. It really does, but I can't. I need to meet with the caterer about opening night."

"This late?"

"She works out of her home and we need to go over some things. Did I tell you I'm hosting a charity toy drive the night of the opening? I'm co-ordinating it with the hospital to help supply the toy bin in Pediatrics and send every child home with a new or gently used toy."

"That's great."

Just then the door to the designated massage room opened and a drowsy looking woman emerged. She paused in the doorway to say her goodbyes. He couldn't see Darcy.

"I've got to go. Nick promised to have my car ready. Give me a call later tonight if you get a chance."

"Uh, yeah, sure. Be careful." He shifted to make it easier for her to give him a kiss.

"Ick. You're all sweaty. Don't muss me for my meeting." She kissed more air than lips, flashed him her practiced smile and then walked away.

Garret glanced back toward the massage room only to find the door closed once more. Swearing beneath his breath at the strange situation he found himself in, he grabbed his gear from the locker room and headed out of the gym.

The February air cooled the sweat on his skin

with numbing swiftness, but that was nothing compared to the surprise he felt when he saw Joss standing outside her car talking to Toby. Joss looked flustered, her normally ultracool persona nowhere to be found as she stared up into Toby's face and gave him what for about something. The scene caught his attention because she looked so fiery and passionate. So *unlike* the woman she was with him. The woman she'd appeared inside the gym. If he wasn't mistaken she almost looked—

Interested in Toby?

The thought came out of nowhere, a sucker punch that couldn't have shocked him more. No way. It was his imagination. One of the first lessons in law school was that in domestic cases the guilty are usually the first to accuse the innocent of their own crimes. The fact he liked Darcy, was curious about her and had been thinking about her as something other than a *friend,* that was why he saw what he thought he saw.

He took a step forward to join them but something held him back. Garret watched, unable to take his eyes off the scene playing out before him. Joss said something he couldn't hear, but Toby's reaction was instantaneous. His buddy bent forward, his head lowering, his posture that of a man about to kiss a woman senseless—or quiet. At the last second, Toby stopped and pulled away, but there was no denying the sexual tension flaring between the two of them.

Had he been played for a fool? Was that why Joss was so uncomfortable of late? Was that why Toby was avoiding his calls? *Guilt?*

Doubts bombarded Garret's head. All those hours he worked. Jocelyn's distance. Tobe stopping by the gallery, pressuring Garret to decide. This was *why?* He ground his teeth until his jawbone popped loud in his ear, angry, furious at Toby's trespassing and yet not sure what to do. The rational, don't-go-off-half-cocked mediator-attorney in him demanded proof before he considered confronting them, and seeing them talking in a parking lot did not qualify as such. But the tension. What about *that?*

Toby stalked off and got into his SUV, peeling out of the parking lot and heading west even though he'd been dressed in work-out clothes and *hadn't* stepped foot inside the gym. Joss did the same but headed east, both of them seemingly trying to stay as far away from each other as possible.

A gust of wind hit him but did nothing for the anger simmering inside him.

Was Joss cheating on him with his best friend?

"Eighteen."

"Twenty-one." Darcy swiped the cards from the couch cushion between them and looked up to find

Garret in the same mood he'd been in all night. No amount of teasing or questions had drawn him out of it. If anything it had gotten darker, his expression more brooding.

The condo was quiet, Rosetta out on a date with one of the men who lived in the building. Garret had scowled when he'd heard the news. He'd hesitated outside the condo door, freshly showered and dressed casually in khaki slacks and a lightweight black sweater that emphasized his good looks, but then asked if he could come in anyway. She hadn't been able to turn him away.

"Ow. Wait a minute, I have to stretch." She made a face and shifted her sideways position on the couch.

"Where's it hurt?"

She smoothed her hand over her lower back and without warning, Garret moved closer until their knees met, putting them face-to-face. Just like that his arms were around her. Despite the surprise of it, she didn't move away. Garret placed his hands on her lower back and began a slow massage.

"Oh, wow." She tried to hold in a moan, but his touch felt too good. "Oh, that feels wonderful."

He chuckled huskily. "You like that, huh?"

Oh, yeah. And he seemed to like it, too. "Don't stop." She tried to hold herself upright and away from Garret's hard, broad chest but the slow push and pull of his hands on her back made that impossible. She dropped her head to his shoulder and closed her eyes with a sigh.

His lips brushed her temple. "How do you do that?"

"Do what?" she whispered, feeling the tension inside her rocketing up by degrees. How was that possible with her the way she was?

"Make me want you when all you're doing is sitting there."

She caught her breath. Seriously? The moist heat of his breath against her neck, her ear, sent shivers through her. "It's all a figment of your imagination. I'm pregnant, or have you forgotten?"

"I haven't forgotten."

Meaning…what? "Garret, stop."

"You said I couldn't." He kissed her temple again. "And I don't want to."

She squeezed her eyes shut at the pitch of his voice. "I don't want to make another mistake. We've spent a lot of time together these past few weeks and it's been fun, but…Garret, you wouldn't be a rebound for me." She lifted her head, looked into his eyes and bared her soul. "This is… It scares me how easy it would be to fall for you." Nothing like a little honesty to send a guy running.

"Would that be a bad thing?"

"Did you and Jocelyn break up?" He shook his head no. "Then, yeah, it would be a bad thing."

"We're close, Darcy. I'm not going to lie to

you. Joss and I never made a verbal agreement to be exclusive, but we have been, almost from the beginning."

She plucked at a button on his shirt, needing something, anything, to do rather than face him. "If you tell me you're one of those guys who says he's in love with two women—"

"I'm not." He lifted her face to his. "Darcy, I'm going to be honest here. I'm not sure what I feel for you. Am I interested? Attracted to you?" He rubbed his thumb over her chin, a slow drag of warmth. "Yes, I am. Does it freak me out that you're pregnant? Yeah. Big time." He smoothed a hand along her jaw until it rested on her nape. "I've thought about marrying Joss for a while now. I bought the ring before Christmas," he admitted softly.

"But something happened?"

He brushed his thumb over her cheek, her mouth, his eyes a turbulent sea. "Yeah…you. You have me thinking things I shouldn't be thinking about a soon-to-be mom."

Garret stared into her eyes, and she saw a reflection of what she felt: a conflict between duty and desire. How often had she wanted to go out and have fun, but was afraid she'd end up like her mother? Afraid she'd end up on the losing end of a string of guys who wanted to get off and nothing else? And when she'd taken the risk, jumped into a relationship with Stephen, look what had happened. How did people know what was right and what was wrong?

"Darcy, say something."

"I know what it's like to want something you don't have. I understand being confused. But I need to know this isn't a joke or a game for you. Whatever *this* is. I understand being confused, but I don't want my heart broken."

"I don't want to break your heart." He settled himself more comfortably against the back of the couch. "I don't want to mislead you, and the last thing I want to do is hurt you, Darcy. I don't know where I stand on a lot of things and you're one of them. All I know is that right now, right here, I'm where I want to be. Is that enough for you for now?"

CHAPTER TWENTY-ONE

HER FANCIFUL IMAGININGS wanted her to think there was a reason she'd had the accident that night. A reason Garret was the one to find her, the one with her now. But she had learned to be a realist. "Why would you want me?"

The question emerged raw, revealed her vulnerability. But her own family didn't want her, why would he? Especially in the condition she was in.

God has the best in store for us, but you have to believe to receive, Darcy. You remember that and you'll have a good life. Nana's voice filled her head, bringing forth a rush of memories and emotions. Rolling out pie crusts on summer afternoons, the radio on an oldies station, Nana in her flowered apron singing "You Are My Sunshine."

But how could she believe in anything—trust in anyone—after what had happened to her with Stephen? After what happened repeatedly to her mother at the hands of the men in her life?

Garret pulled her close, kissed her gently, his

mouth lingering on hers. "Because you're you," he murmured against her lips. "Because you look me in the eyes and you're honest with me about what you feel. Honesty is…hot."

She laughed at him. At them. "I'm scared of screwing up."

"Me, too."

There it was again, that fairy-tale feeling. Why was she doing this to herself?

"You are the last thing I expected to enter my life at this point, but I'm glad you did," he said.

She nuzzled her nose against him. "This is crazy messed up. You know that, don't you? I'm *huge*. My back hurts, my ankles are puffy and I should *not* be thinking about you this way."

"But you are?" Garret's eyes warmed with blatant interest. In the space of a heartbeat an arrested expression crossed his face, one of hunger and excitement and curiosity that made her body tighten in response. "Come here." He snagged her with a hand behind her nape and kissed her. Not the sweet, chaste kisses of before, but hungry, urgent, drowning get-to-know-what-you-like-best strokes that turned her muscles to mush.

Darcy moaned, unprepared for the onslaught of desire Garret unleashed, and found herself gently pulled upward onto her knees and shifted about, until she was draped across his lap and well able to feel the steely strength of his arousal against her hip. Oh, yeah, he wasn't kidding her. That couldn't be faked.

Garret raised his head briefly as though to check to make sure she was okay, but when she didn't utter a complaint he kissed her again, using his teeth to nip, his tongue to soothe, delving inside to explore. He didn't rush her and she knew if she were to protest, Garret would immediately stop. But she didn't want him to. No, she wound her arms around his neck and kissed him back, shivering when his broad palm slipped from her thigh to her breast and squeezed.

"Beautiful. Do you have any idea how many times I thought about doing this?"

Yes. Because she'd dreamed of him doing it more than once. This morning she'd donned a baby-doll style dress, scoop-necked at the top and loose around her belly, the bottom of which reached midthigh, and lace-trimmed leggings beneath, and now she relished her choice when the material posed little barrier to Garret as he smoothed his hand back down her body to her knee, up again. When he reached her shoulder he dragged his knuckles along her collarbone, into her cleavage and then slipped beneath the material and her bra to cup her again, this time flesh to flesh.

"*Oh.*" Her breasts had never been all that sensitive, but with her pregnancy they were. And the feel of him touching her— "Garret, please."

"You're killing me, sweetheart." He kissed her mouth, her cheek, her neck, following the course of his hand, all the while giving her gentle little scrapes of his thumb. Back and forth, so slow. The arm supporting her back tightened, lifting her toward him and she held her breath, waiting for the moment his lips touched her, laved and sucked with all the pent-up hunger she felt radiating from him. The shock of it shot straight to her core, and she stiffened before curling into him, desperate for more.

Garret groaned. "Beautiful." Still holding her so that he could play with her breasts, he slid his hand to her knee and raised it, settling her foot on the couch just so, before he went back to what he was doing. Touching, tasting, making her gasp and moan, his decadent mouth on her throat, her chest, his free hand meandering up and down her body and leaving a blazing trail behind. What was he doing to her?

Garret's heart thudded beneath her ear, his breathing unsteady, proof that he was enjoying himself and wasn't simply going through the motions or doing this for her. He wanted to, because he wanted her. Amazing. Dangerous to her heart, but amazing all the same.

A rough sound escaped him, a growl, a chest-deep rumble, and he shifted so that she laid more fully across his lap, more open to his touch. His hand slipped lower, inward on her thighs, between.

"Garret."

He cupped her, the thin barrier of her leggings not protecting her from the heat of his thumb, each movement sending a sizzle of excitement through her until she could scarcely keep from crying out. Over and over he touched her, kissed, rubbed, his mouth on hers long enough to capture her moans before moving on, lower, focusing on her breasts since they brought her pleasure—a devastating suck and stroke that made her writhe. If someone had said she could feel like this now…

Then Garret's hand found exactly the right spot. "There." He kissed her, hard and fast and sexy rough, his breath hitting her cheek when he broke contact to laugh softly. "Ah, yeah, sweetheart, right there. I love the look on your face."

He repeated the motion, varying the pressure and angle of his touch until she clutched his shoulders, kissing him, desperate, for more. Harder, faster, *more.* Whimpering, moaning, struggling to breathe as Garret built the tension inside her body to an un-bearable degree. Finally, oh, *finally,* he cupped his hand around her and pressed, palming her and taking her mouth with his as he ground his hand against her until she shattered, her soft scream of pleasure captured by his mouth.

Darcy laid sprawled on his lap afterward, her nose buried in Garret's neck. Doubts, fears, total embarrassment bombarded her, but she shoved all the emotions aside to enjoy the moment, knowing she felt more for Garret than she ever had for Stephen. How scary was that? How sad? She'd known Garret a matter of weeks and yet he meant more to her than her baby's father? What did that say about her?

But it was true. She'd spent almost every evening talking with Garret, getting to know him, and what they'd just shared? It was nothing short of… magical.

Which made it all the more terrifying.

Garret shifted his hand between her thighs and aftershocks rolled through her. He made himself more comfortable on the couch, holding her on his lap, silent.

What was he thinking? Did he regret what they'd just done? Shoving those thoughts aside, she brushed her lips over his jaw, his throat, moving lower, shifting to have better access to his clothing.

"Darcy, no."

"But—"

"Gram will be home soon." He held her hands, bussed his lips against her forehead. "You were beautiful. This was wonderful. But I should go."

Tears pricked her eyelids and she blinked rapidly. "I know." But she didn't want it to end. Didn't want reality to intrude even though it was crashing back in drowning waves. She was too impulsive. She shouldn't have let things go so far, shouldn't have been so eager, but—

Garret hugged her close and raised her head with a hand under her chin, his mouth finding hers with unerring accuracy. And just like that her heart kicked up speed, the trembling started deep inside.

"I don't want to hurt you, Darcy. I'd never deliberately hurt you. Whatever happens, will you please remember that?"

And there it was. Reality. He wanted her to remember that—if he chose Jocelyn?

When, not *if.* "I'll try."

"YOU'RE AWFULLY QUIET. Something happen back at the gym?"

Nick's voice startled Darcy from her thoughts. She hadn't been able to concentrate all day. All she could think about was Garret and what had happened between them last night.

Was she more like her mother than she thought? A few pretty words and she gave in? She glanced over her shoulder and saw Matt in the backseat playing a handheld game, oblivious to the adults thanks to the earphones tucked in his ears. Would she have a boy like Matt? A little girl? What kind of shape would she be in when she gave birth if she let herself fall for Garret only to be cast aside?

Getting closer to Garret had seemed like a wonderful idea last night, but in the harsh light of day—*Face it, you acted just like Mom.*

She settled herself against the seat and tried to stave off the upset and embarrassment. She'd never done that before, gotten so close to a guy so soon after meeting. Stephen had said he'd practically had to pry her thighs apart and that was after dating him nearly six months. She didn't do easy, didn't do one-night stands, didn't feel like she owed a guy anything just because he bought her dinner. So why did she want to do all those things and more with Garret?

"Darcy?"

"Do you ever wonder," she asked softly, "if you're making the right decisions?"

Nick smiled. "Only every day. Are you talking about parenting or something else?"

"Life in general. I want…I want whatever happens next to be right for both me and the baby. And I really need it to happen quickly given, well, this," she said, indicating her belly. "Rosetta says I'll go into labor soon because I've cleaned the apartment from top to bottom and washed everything that wasn't attached to something."

Nick chuckled as he drove her home to the condo. "I remember Matt's mom doing that."

She glanced at Matt again. The child was oblivious

to their conversation but she lowered her voice to be sure. "What happened? If you don't mind my asking?"

Thirty seconds passed before he shrugged. "She had stars in her eyes at the thought of being a Tulane and moving to the top of the mountain. When she realized I wasn't going to go crawling back to my parents and marrying me meant she was just going to get me, she left. But she left the best thing between us behind." He cleared his throat, his jaw locking and unlocking at his thoughts. "It hasn't been easy, but kids are resilient, Darcy. They'll love you no matter how screwed up things get sometimes."

She let that pass without comment. She loved her mother because she was her mother, but a deep, caring love? If not for Nana's love until her passing and a deep-rooted sense of right and wrong she wouldn't know *how* to love her baby. Her mom hadn't taught her that. But was her version of love dark and twisted? Was it the *right way* to love or was it only a matter of time before she screwed that up, too? "Do you think your parents regret not being close to you?" The question slipped out before she could stop it. "I can't believe I asked that. How rude, Nick, I'm sorry. My mom and I are— We have a lot of problems, and I'm worried they'll carry over and come between me and my baby. That the pattern will repeat. I didn't mean to sound insensitive about you and your family."

"It's okay. And the answer is yes. I do, too. But I can't see them making any other decision at the time." He grimaced. "I did the right thing by leaving, they did the right thing by setting down an example for my brothers and sister. Who's right? Some people need distance to be themselves and I'm one of them. Maybe you are, too. Things are undeniably tense and awkward when I'm with my family, but short visits work well. Usually no one gets hurt that way."

She smiled sadly. Would short visits work with her mother? *Only if she'd want to see you.* Who wanted to live their life that way? Waiting for a phone call from her mother to say it was okay to come visit? A phone call that probably would only come when her mother was between men, canceled at the last minute if the guy came back or a new one entered? No, she wasn't going to do that, put her child through the drama. She had to build relationships and connections on her own, for them both.

With a man who wasn't sure where he wanted to be?

"No matter how hard you try, you can't live for other people. You have to be your own person first, a person you can live with so that whoever you're involved with can't make or break your happiness."

Wise advice. Until the baby came and she recovered, she was stuck in town with Garret. That was a given. But what about afterward? What did a person do when she was sure what the right decision was but wasn't ready to make it?

"GARRET, we need to talk." Harry bulldozed his way into the office and shut the door.

Garret set the supply report aside and frowned at his boss. "I didn't think you were coming in today. Something wrong?"

"Yes, something is wrong. You listen to me and listen good. You know I'm not a patient man, and I've had enough of this Darcy person and the talk that's going around. Whatever it is that has you going over there nearly every night to see that woman won't last."

"Darcy is on her own and doesn't know anyone in town. You can't sympathize with that?"

"Don't give me that bull. That may have been true when she first arrived, but she knows plenty of people now. I know about her working for Nick, and isn't that supposedly *why* she's staying with Rosetta? As her companion?" he demanded pointedly. "She doesn't need you babysitting her. Joss is—"

"Joss and I have discussed this, Harry, and she's okay with it." He couldn't say that *they* were okay because they weren't, but the last thing he'd do was discuss his suspicions with Harry. He wasn't sure whom to confront first. Joss, Tobe. Or himself. Had too many hours working and his friendship with Darcy pushed Joss into Toby's arms?

People cheat because they want to, no one makes them.

And before he could throw stones he had to take a hard look at what he'd done with Darcy last night. That factored in, too. Complicated things more.

"I don't want you seeing that woman."

"I'll see whomever I damn well please."

"Then you're a fool. She's taking advantage of you and you're blind to it. Just like you've always been to Richardson hanging on to your family's coattails."

He left the subject of Toby alone. "Darcy hasn't asked for a thing from me. If anything I have to make her accept my help because she doesn't like charity."

Harry growled. "I'll prove to you what kind of person she is. All I have to do is offer her some money and you'll see how fast she runs with it."

He stood but didn't move from behind the desk, knowing it gave him the position of power in the room. Two could play Harry's hard ball. "Stay away from her. Darcy isn't like that, and if you upset her, you'll answer for it."

"To who? You?"

He smirked. "I won't have to say a word. Think my grandmother will let you get by with tormenting a pregnant woman in her care?"

"She needs to go."

"Go *where?* Darcy can't travel."

"There are ways. I'll *hire* someone to drive her out of here if I have to."

"Harry, I mean it. You keep your foul moods away from her. Upsetting Darcy could send her into labor."

"If it means she'd leave sooner, that would be a good thing. Garret, fix this. You end it now or else."

"What are you saying?"

"Do you really think your job will survive, treating my daughter this way? Think your brother will get that promotion if this continues?"

"Now you're resorting to *threats?*"

"Take it however you like," the man drawled. "The gallery opening is in three weeks. The place will be crawling with reporters and people ready for a party, and I expect you to help give them one. Propose to Jocelyn beforehand and let the damn opening night of that nightmare be for something meaningful. After dragging her along for years, she deserves a special evening. In the meantime, stay away from that pregnant tramp or I'll see to it you aren't left standing."

Garret watched Harry leave, all the anger and frustration inside him reaching critical mass. He was sick of this. Sick of the drama, the godlike haul-ass-and-get-it-done-now-or-else behavior Harry had displayed for the past couple years. Sick of it all.

He sat and stared out the window, not giving a flying leap about the supply lists or contracts on his desk, not even the one he'd worked so hard to get. He'd crashed and burned a long time ago, he just hadn't wanted to face it.

"Deep thoughts for such a beautiful day." Gram regarded him from the doorway, concern in her eyes. "I take it Harry is on another rampage?"

Normally he would've brushed her off with a smile, laugh and firm no comment, but he didn't. He shoved himself upright, deciding Harry could review the contract if he wanted nurses working the hospital in the near future. "Want to go get some coffee?"

A smile lit her features. "I'd love to."

Fifteen minutes later they were in a coffee shop off main street, the place mostly empty because of the time of day.

"Harry's applying pressure, is he?" Gram murmured.

"You could say that."

"Did something happen between you and Darcy?"

His head jerked up. "Why do you ask?"

Gram smiled in that knowing way she had. "Because she's looking much the same way you do. I know the two of you are getting close. I can tell. And I'm worried about you. Both of you."

He stared into the murky depths of his drink. "We were just friends, but now—" How could he describe how he felt?

"Now you're more? Is that wise considering the relationship you already have in your life?"

"No. I can't say that it is. I'm…confused, Gram."

"Darcy is a wonderful girl. She'd make any man a good wife."

"But so is Joss," he added.

"Very true."

"You're not helping me here, Gram." He took a sip of the coffee he didn't want. "Harry wants me to propose to Joss the night of the gallery opening. Make it a big to-do." He couldn't look at her.

"Is that what you want?"

"I want…peace. I want things to settle down with my job and with Harry on a rampage all the time and me doing his job and mine, I can't find it unless—"

"Unless what?"

He'd been about to say *unless I'm with Darcy* but would Gram understand? How could she when *he* didn't? "Joss is a good woman. We're good together and I love her. I do love her."

"I know."

"Three years is a long time to wait, but she has and she's been patient. She's been fantastic. She hasn't pressured me, has stood by me working long hours and weekends. But lately things have been… strained, and I'm wondering if it's time to fish or cut bait."

"Because you're interested in Darcy now, too?"

He didn't answer right away. Wasn't about to mention what he'd seen to Gram. If he did marry Joss, he didn't want Gram suspicious of Joss every time she saw her talking to Toby. *It was nothing. They were just talking—you are the one who's crossed the line.* "With Darcy I feel…different." He made himself meet her gaze. "I want what you and Grandpa had, Gram. But how do I know which one is *the* one when both of them would make me happy?"

Gram dabbed at her eyes with a napkin.

"I'm sorry. All I've done is upset you. I should've known you'd—"

"No, Garret. No, that's not it. Some people go their entire lives never finding someone to love. You've been blessed with two wonderful women."

"Joss is great and we're good together, but how do I know good couldn't be better?"

"Darcy?"

He managed a nod. "I don't want to hurt either one of them."

"Then I suggest you figure out where you stand and quickly," she told him, "because the longer you drag this out, the worse someone is going to be hurt."

CHAPTER TWENTY-TWO

THE WEEK of Rosetta's birthday party passed with surprising swiftness, but with it came more anxiety and stress. Darcy sighed. Trying to protect herself was impossible. It was too late for that. So she simply tried to take the days one at a time and distract herself from the fact that Garret had distanced himself from her.

Twice during the week she'd overdone things at the gym and needed to take the medicine to end the cramping. A little rest and she was back on her feet again, even though she could barely see them. Garret called three times to check on her, claiming work kept him away. She wasn't convinced, and came to the conclusion that he regretted what they'd shared on the couch, just like he'd regretted the kiss in her bedroom, which made her all the more embarrassed by her behavior. And angry. At him, at herself.

Garret didn't come to see her and Rosetta as he had before. Was he spending the time with Jocelyn? What were they doing? Did he touch Jocelyn the way he'd touched her?

Jealousy sucked. How did women *do* this? Here she was going to have a baby, for pity's sake. The timing couldn't have been worse for her to meet Garret, but she had and it was too late. She cared for him. Wanted him—and he wasn't hers to want.

"Something wrong, dear?"

Darcy started and realized she'd been staring into space. She finished drying the plate she held. "Just thinking about how giving my clients have been. The gifts and all. It won't be easy to pack up. I'll have to rent a U-Haul to move everything."

"You're thinking of moving? Not staying?"

"Why would I stay?"

"Well, there's plenty of time to decide. And plenty of places around town to live if you change your mind about making Beauty your home. Not that I'm in a hurry for you to leave. I like having you here."

"Yeah, well, if Nick continues at the current pace on my car, I'll never be able to move." Rosetta looked away and busied herself scrubbing an already-clean counter. "Did you tell him to do it at snail speed?"

She knew she was right in her thinking when Rosetta had the grace to blush. The two-week time frame had come and gone—three weeks ago.

"I'll only admit to suggesting to him that I was afraid if he got the work done right away, you might decide to ignore doctor's orders and drive on alone."

Darcy inhaled and sighed once more. She'd decided to do just that a million times over, but common sense prevailed when she remembered what it was like to be stuck at the side of the road in labor.

"We both agreed it was a good idea to…delay things a bit. Are you upset with me, dear?"

She put the plate away and grabbed another, careful not to drip on her dress. "No. It's sweet that you care so much. Rosetta, I'll never be able to repay you for all you've done for me."

"You've done as much or more for me, Darcy. You've been a wonderful friend and I don't like the idea of you out there alone. I like watching over you. I've come to think of you as family."

That was the problem. It was becoming all too easy to pretend the Tulane family *was* hers. Rosetta's grandmotherly love and support was so precious, so reminiscent of Nana. Darcy liked the feeling of being watched over, too. Nick and Ethan, they were the brothers she'd never had. And Garret— Her feelings for him could only deepen at this point. A useless act since they could only develop so far. A week of his keeping his distance was proof of that.

"Darcy?" Rosetta's face softened. "Oh, honey. You're falling in love with him, aren't you?"

"No." Denial was automatic, a built-in life preserver. "No, I'm not." It was time to grow up. For her baby's sake, if not her own. Which meant not becoming any more involved with a man destined to marry another woman.

A sharp knock sounded on the condo door before it opened and closed, ending their conversation.

She turned away from Rosetta, putting the last plate away and trying to brace herself for the barrage of feelings overwhelming her. She wasn't falling. She'd *fallen.* Hard, fast. How could she have allowed it to happen? Staying in Beauty was temporary. *Garret* was temporary. How awkward was it going to be to meet the infamous Jocelyn Pierson, caretaker of the hospital's poor and underprivileged? How difficult would it be to look the other woman in the eye knowing Garret had kissed *her?*

He might've kissed you, but where has he been?

She heard heavy footfalls enter the kitchen and her heart picked up speed. If Garret gave her that look, she'd know everything would be all right but— She turned to see Ethan smiling at them both. "Wow. You two look hot."

Ethan had come to pick them up. Not Garret.

Because he would escort his girlfriend *to the party, not you.*

Darcy clutched the countertop, closed her eyes briefly. What *was* she thinking? *Doing?* She had a baby to care for, a life to build, and here she was thinking about a man? What about her baby? Garret had turned her into—

"Are you all right, Darcy?"

"I'm fine."

"You look a little pale." Ethan frowned at her, wearing his doctor face. "Are you sure you're up for this?"

She saw the gentle warning in his eyes, as if he was well aware of what was going through her mind. Rosetta, now Ethan. They'd known all along what she hadn't been able to see. The gossip was true. She'd become the other woman.

Somehow she managed to pin a weak smile to her lips, her stomach in knots. "Let's get this party started."

Because the sooner it was over, the sooner it was *all* over, the sooner she could leave.

Joss smoothed a hand over her dress and frowned at the Jeep they neared. "Isn't that Tobias's?"

Garret shot her a glance, then shrugged. "Yeah. Why do you ask?"

"No reason. You'd said the party was mostly going to be family and friends, that's all."

"Toby's a friend. You don't think so?"

"Of course. I spoke without thinking." Or had she? Was this the beginning of her filling her father's shoes?

They continued on, entered the large double doors leading into the Tulane family home.

"There he is. Let's go."

Her head snapped up, her gaze immediately locking on Tobias. He'd been watching them.

"I see a friend I need to speak to." Jocelyn dug her four-inch heels into the opulent carpet. "I'll join you in a minute."

Garret's gaze sharpened. "Something wrong?"

"No. Why would you think that?"

Before he could answer she saw Garret's attention leave her. She followed his gaze and found Ethan escorting Rosetta and her pregnant guest into the room. So this was Darcy Rhodes.

She wished the woman was prettier. Not that Darcy was ugly by any means. But she was *attractive,* not beautiful, which made Garret's talk-of-the-town friendship with her all the more disturbing. Was something going on between them? "We need to say hello to your grandmother and wish her a happy birthday." She didn't know why she said it. She didn't want to meet Darcy face-to-face and knew that to walk over there she forced them both into a slew of speculation. But she didn't care. No, there was a recklessness taking hold inside her, one that had grown every day since she'd broken all the rules and kissed Garret's best friend.

"If you like."

Joss fell into step beside Garret and forced her chin high, aware that Tobias's mocking gaze followed.

THREE HOURS after the string band played "Happy Birthday" for Rosetta's arrival, Darcy accepted the cake handed to her by one of the catering staff and looked around for a quiet spot. Not finding any nearby, she escaped the crowded main rooms and made her way down a hallway. Spying an open, darkened room, she slipped inside and collapsed into the closest chair, her nerves raw, her emotions under a thin thread of control.

Garret's parents were warm and welcoming and had made her feel very much a part of things despite the questions she saw in their expressions. Garret's family was... awesome. They hugged and congratulated each other over the slightest accomplishments, complimented each other, missed each other. Only Nick stood off to the side, listening, watching it all, the quietest of the bunch, speaking when spoken to and obviously on edge.

Worse, her feet hurt, her back hurt and she felt totally inferior and out of place in her bargain-basement maternity dress compared to Garret's gorgeous girlfriend. She wore Vera Wang on her size-four body and wore it well.

Meeting Jocelyn had been just as painful and awkward as she'd feared. Another eye-opening smack to the face because she and Garret looked so perfect together. If not for Rosetta's presence at her side, she would've left then and there. Maybe it was a good thing Nick hadn't returned her car because had she had it, she would've jumped inside and driven to the next town at least. Anything to establish some distance.

Sighing, she propped the cake on her built-in belly tray and closed her eyes, concentrating on relaxing her tense muscles in the hopes that the cramping she'd felt off and on all night would fade. The last thing she wanted to do was ruin someone's enjoyment of Rosetta's party by having to ask for a ride back to the condo. Or the hospital.

Multiple footsteps approached the room where she sat. *Keep walking. Don't come in, keep walking. Please.* She needed a moment alone to regain her composure.

"For the last time, go away and leave me alone."

"You can't *talk* to me?"

Darcy recognized the voice of Garret's girlfriend and Toby Richardson. She shrank down in the high-backed chair, wanting to disappear.

"What are you doing, Tobias? Do you want people talking about us? I've had enough gossip these past few weeks."

Darcy winced, her guilt growing.

"Then what's a little more? Stop treating me like the plague."

"I'm marrying Garret."

"If he asks."

"He's going to. He told Daddy that he planned to ask the night of the gallery opening."

Her throat closed. So that was it. That explained Garret's absence. He'd felt guilty about their make-out session, he'd made his decision and that was that, wasn't it?

Darcy lifted a hand to her mouth. Jocelyn's announcement was proof positive that she had to get out of there. Out of Rosetta's condo. Out of Beauty. Far, far away.

"When are you going to see what a mistake this is?"

A mistake? Darcy waited for Jocelyn's answer, holding her breath when a cramp sharpened and became uncomfortable. She squirmed in the seat.

"It's *not* a mistake."

"He's interested in someone else. You're just going to overlook that? Do you really think that little stunt you pulled, having Garret introduce you to her, fooled anyone?"

"It's your motives that are suspect, Tobias. What if he'd seen you that night in the parking lot? Walked out and heard the things you were saying to me? He was right inside the gym."

What night?

"We were talking. What was he doing that night?"

"What do you mean?"

"He went to her. I drove around for a while to cool off, and since I was curious to see if he was with you, I drove by Rosetta's. Garret was there. The thing is, I kept driving and ran into Rosetta. She was out with friends. They'd been to a movie, had dinner. Which means Darcy and Garret were in the condo alone. If you love him so much, are you going to stand there and tell me that doesn't bother you?"

Darcy fisted her hands, trapped, angry and hurting. Garret had come to see her that night because—

It doesn't matter. You're leaving anyway. Soon as the baby is born, you're outta here. Why does it matter?

Because it hurt so much. She'd sensed Garret's upset that night. His distraction and unwillingness to talk about whatever had put him in his brooding mood. Now she knew why. Her face burned with anger and embarrassment. Garret had given her pleasure and not taken any for himself, but she still felt used. As if she were the toy he'd played with because the one he wanted wasn't available.

"No. No, it doesn't bother me. He's her friend, just her friend."

Just her friend. Of all the people to forget that fact, why did it have to be her?

"You're really going to do this? You're going to marry him because Daddy says so?"

"I'm going to marry Garret because I love him. Nothing you say can change that."

Darcy closed her eyes.

"Now be a true friend to Garret and me both, Tobias. Leave us alone."

The sound of Jocelyn's heels faded as she continued on her way down the tiled hall. Darcy stayed where she was, unmoving. Another pain slid around her stomach, harder than the one before.

The gallery opening was two weeks from today. Which meant she had to leave town before then.

Toby cursed, then shoved open the door, startling her. The light above her head flicked on, and she winced at the blinding brightness, grimacing as she waited to see if she would be discovered.

He stalked over to the wet bar at the far side of the study, poured himself a drink and turned, spotting her immediately. He froze, the glass halfway to his lips. "Aw, hell."

Darcy set the forgotten cake aside, managing to get to her feet without too much trouble.

"Darcy, wait."

"Why? Does anything really need to be said?" She rubbed her back in slow, hard circles, thankful for once her body was cooperating. Two weeks was plenty of time to recover. At least enough to get out of town.

"I'm sorry."

Another contraction began, slow and insidious, spreading around her, through her, becoming sharp and piercing. She bit her lip, closed her eyes.

"Please don't tell me— No way. I just went through this with my sister," he complained.

The comment made her laugh despite the tears setting her throat on fire. "Traumatized you, did it?"

"You could say that." Toby set the drink on the bar and hurried toward her. "Need a ride? I know a back way out of here. If you're interested?"

"Definitely."

"Think you can make it around the porch to the front? If so, I'll meet you there with your coat."

She didn't move until the contraction passed. "Yes. I…I can do that. But don't tell anyone. I don't want to ruin the party."

"No problem. Let's go."

Toby showed her the French doors that opened out onto a wraparound porch. She headed toward the front of the house slowly, careful to watch her step on the moisture-slicked planks, thankful for the moon lighting the way around expensive outdoor furniture and planters. Darcy rounded the corner of the house only to pause. Garret sat sprawled on a bench staring up at the night sky.

He heard her and turned, immediately shoved himself to his feet. "What are you doing?"

"Leaving."

"Where's your coat? Are you feeling all right? What happened?"

"I'm fine. I just want to go ho— To the condo.

Please give Rosetta my best and tell her I'm tired. I'll see her in the morning."

"Don't leave." He shrugged his suit jacket off and wrapped it around her. "I'll take you upstairs. You can lie down in one of the bedrooms. If you're not feeling well, you shouldn't be alone."

She shrugged the coat off and handed it back to him. "Thanks, but no. And I won't be alone. Your friend Toby is driving me."

"Toby?" He tossed the jacket aside. "Why are you going with *Toby?*"

"He's leaving. He's going to drop me off on his way home."

He took another step closer. "Are you sure that's it? Where were you? I've been looking for you. I wanted to tell you something."

"I— In the bathroom. Pregnant women, you know?"

"Darcy, what's going on? Did someone say something to you?"

"No. No one said a thing to me. In fact, everyone has been amazingly nice, considering."

"Considering what?"

"Considering who I am. I see where you get your kindness and manners. Your parents are great. And Jocelyn is— She's beautiful. I heard about what she's doing for the children's ward at the hospital, using the gallery opening to get donations. That's sweet. You're going to be happy with her."

Garret stiffened. "What did you say?" He grasped her elbow and gently tugged her deeper into the shadows along the side of the porch.

Embarrassed to be seen with her?

"You're upset." He swore softly. "Darcy, I'm sorry about this week. Work has been a nightmare with Harry arguing every change, and I thought, given timing, it might be good for both of us to take a breather and make sure we're doing the right thing."

"It was perfect timing," she agreed. His expression softened into one that tugged at her heart-strings—until they broke.

"If this is about me not picking you up tonight—"

"Of course not. I mean, why would you bring me? I'm not your girlfriend. Or should I say fiancée?"

CHAPTER TWENTY-THREE

SEEING GARRET GRIMACE at her wording didn't make Darcy feel any better.

"This hasn't been fair to you or Jocelyn."

"You're right. Which is why I'm going to do what I should've done from the beginning—keep my distance and ask that you keep yours." She shook her head when he opened his mouth. "I mean it, Garret. This week, tonight, helped me realize I've turned into someone I *swore* I'd never be—the other woman." She laughed, the sound bitter to her own ears. "My mother may be on husband number four, but it's not for lack of trying to get other women's husbands to notice her. I know better than to think situations like this end happily. It's ironic to think of myself as a homewrecker, big as I am, but it's true. That's what they consider me, too. The people in there."

"You're—"

"You care for me. I know that, I can see it in your face. It's not enough. This isn't what I want."

"Stop. Before you say anything else, hear me out. I—"

"I can't *do* this! No matter what you say right now, no matter how you look at me or make me *feel*, I can't handle a baby and a relationship. Especially one like ours would be."

"How would it *be?* Are you saying you won't even give me a chance?"

"It would be awful." She waved a hand to indicate the house. "I've been in there wandering around all night, listening to everyone talk about you and her and how soon you'll be married. They're all excited about it. Then there were the whispers about me that would stop when I got near. They love you, Garret. They're concerned about you." She smiled up at him, the effort costing her more than he'd ever know. "I didn't want to like her but I did. Jocelyn could've been really mean and hateful toward me because of all the talk, because of what we've *done*."

"Darcy—"

"But she wasn't. She went out of her way to be nice, and that only made me feel worse." Now she knew why Melanie irritated Scarlett O'Hara so much. All that goodness and kindness was hard to take.

"You're both nice. You're both beautiful and friendly but that's what made this—"

"Garret, *stop*. She was *nice*. Three years is too long a time to date someone only to throw it away when someone like me crashes into town and gets your attention by foisting myself on you. That's all it was, too. You reached out to me, connected with me, because you thought I was safe. I'm pregnant, passing through. I was someone you could talk to. Mess around with."

"Dammit, Darcy, it wasn't like that." Garret stepped close, but she backed away. He stopped with a low growl of frustration. "You're more than that. Darcy, you have every right to doubt me, to be scared, but I need you to hear me. I've made this situation worse by being so indecisive, but I needed to bring Jocelyn tonight. I felt like I owed her that because—"

"Doesn't that tell you something? Because it tells me what I need to hear, loud and clear. Garret, I have to put my baby first. And I'm doing it tonight."

"Don't do this. Not now. I just need a little more time."

"Whatever we had is over, Garret."

Darcy shook her head, tried to ignore the cramp growing stronger, taking her ability to breathe normally.

"Darcy?" His gaze narrowed. "Darcy, are you—"

The door opened behind them. "Darcy?" Toby's low murmur couldn't have come at a better time.

"I'm h-here." She needed help. Knew she couldn't walk away from Garret on her own.

"I'm taking you to the hospital."

"*No.*"

"Dammit, Darcy—"

"Stop swearing at her," Toby ordered, moving to her side.

"Tobe, stay out of this."

The contraction finally ended and she released the breath she held in a gush. "Don't talk to him like that. At least Toby knows what he wants."

Toby helped her into her coat. "Come on."

"No. Darcy, wait."

She laughed, surprising both men if their expressions were any indication. "I said that to you," she told Garret. "The night you found me in the snow. Now I wish you had kept driving."

"You don't mean that."

"Yeah, I do. My baby deserves the best I can give it, and that means being with someone who can put us first. I refuse to be second anymore. I can't be my mother, Garret. Not even for you."

"You're not your mother, sweetheart. You're scared because you've convinced yourself the only person you can rely on is yourself, but that's not true. Don't do this. I needed some time to think, but I know what I want now. I know I want *you*, Darcy."

Pain coursed through her, but whether it was from the contractions or her heart shattering, she wasn't sure. "No, you don't. You want what you can't have," she whispered, struggling to hold her head high. "Goodbye, Garret. Be happy."

"Darcy, don't do this. Not now. Let me come with you."

She shook her head, sad, terrified, afraid she was broken inside where it mattered most.

Toby wrapped an arm around her back and helped her to his Jeep. Darcy stared out the window at Garret's imposing form looking so masculine against the wide white columns of the house, the image bringing back more memories of the first night she'd met him. Tears blurred her eyes but she didn't let them fall. She'd cried enough. Now it was time to be strong.

As Toby drove her down the mountain to the hospital, her contractions began to hit closer together, harder, more intense. *Oh, Nana, I need help. Why aren't you here?*

"You okay?"

"You stared at her all night," she whispered. "I saw you watching her and wondered…before I ever heard what you said. Do you love her, too?"

Toby didn't pretend to not know what or who she was talking about. "Yeah. What about you and Garret?"

"Yeah."

"Fine mess we got ourselves into, isn't it?"

She wrapped her hands around her rock-hard stomach. *Mama loves you.* "Yeah."

GARRET PULLED Joss out of the crowded house and onto the porch.

"Garret? Where have you been? I haven't seen you for over an hour."

"Darcy's in labor."

The words made her blanch. Already pale, she turned positively ghostlike. Before Darcy had found him he'd sat here and reviewed everything in his head. Three years of dates with Joss—laughs, sex, holidays and vacations spent together. Family gatherings like the one tonight. The feeling of dissatisfaction he'd felt for too long. The scene in the gym's parking lot. All of it jumbled up inside his head, combining with the time he'd spent with Darcy. The way she smelled, laughed. Her heart of gold and the kindness she'd shown toward others in little ways. Extra time working at the massage table because someone had had a bad day, the way she jumped up to help Gram when he knew Darcy had to be hurting and uncomfortable. The way she'd welcomed him into her arms, was honest about her feelings. Her fears. What had he done? Why had he waited so long?

Straightening, he turned around and took Joss into his arms. Her eyes widened when he palmed her face and brought her mouth to his, kissing her for all he was worth. Lips, teeth, tongue, seductive strokes and all the finesse he had in him. After a moment he lifted his head and watched her closely.

But other than blinking her eyes open and giving him a weak smile, his kiss had garnered no more passion than a brotherly kiss on the cheek. More proof of what he already knew.

"Garret, what's wrong?"

"Do you love me?"

She hesitated a split second. "Of course I do."

"No." His hands fell to her shoulders. "Do you *love* me? Are you *in love* with me? Do you imagine the two of us together for the next *fifty* years? Day after day, night after night? Do you dream about me making love to you?"

"Garret, I—"

"Do. You. *Love*. Me?" He shook her gently. "Do *you* want to marry me, or are you simply doing what you think you're supposed to do? What we're supposed to do because it's been three years and everybody says it's the next step?"

She inhaled a sharp gasp. "*What?* You're asking me this now? *Here?*"

"I need to hear you say it. I wouldn't hurt you for the world, but I need to hear you tell me you love me, that you can't imagine living your life without me. Because if you can't say it, we both know something's wrong."

"You're making this about *me* when it's…it's really about you. Can *you* say it?"

He didn't want to hurt her. "No."

"Because of Darcy."

"Because I need more from my wife than you're willing to give. When I kiss you, touch you, what do you feel? I just kissed you and you looked bored by it. Are you going to stand there and say you want *years* together after that kind of response? That you haven't pulled away from me lately because you're not feeling me?"

She opened her mouth, but other than trembling lips and the sound of her breath panting, no sound came for a long, long time. "Garret, I…" A tear trickled down her cheek. "I care for you. *So much.* I'd do anything for you. You are such a good man and a wonderful friend. My best friend. I never wanted to hurt you or endanger your position with my father because I *know* how he can be, but I don't—"

"Love me? Not like that? Not like a *husband?*"

Trembling from head to toe, she shook her head.

"Thank God. I don't love you, either. I do—" he dropped a kiss to her forehead "—love you, but not like a wife."

She looked as shell-shocked as he felt. "Oh, Garret. How did we let this happen? How did we let it come this far?"

"I guess at the time, no one else made us stop to take notice. Now they have."

She smoothed a trembling hand over her hair.

"We've been together so long. Like everyone else, I thought we were it. I couldn't stand to hurt you, and Daddy never let up about us getting married. I didn't want to ruin things at the hospital or your relationship with him after all this time. It sounds so fatalistic now, but—"

He hugged her close. "I know. Joss, I was going to do the same thing."

Her arms surrounded him, held tight. "What are we going to do? What happens next?"

"I'll go along with whatever you tell people. Whatever you want to tell Harry."

She exhaled roughly. "Daddy is going to be furious with us both. Oh, this is a nightmare. And right before the *opening*. Oh, no."

Garret moved back far enough to lift her chin with his hand. "Blame me. Tell him I'm a jerk who strung you along, tell him anything you want. Just know Darcy and I haven't slept together. This isn't about her. It's about us not living the lives we want."

Her lashes fell over her eyes. "I kissed someone else. Once."

He grinned, knowing without a doubt who that person was and unable to believe the mess they'd both have been in if he'd done as ordered and proposed. He bussed the top of her head and squeezed her tight once more. "You're the best,

Joss, but I have to go. I have to get Gram and go to the hospital. Darcy can't have the baby alone."

"No. No, of course not."

Garret released her, then hesitated. "I don't know if Darcy will forgive me for making such a mess of things, but this is a lesson for both of us, you know. Maybe you could make this the night you stand up to your father and go after Toby."

Her eyes widened, her mouth parting in a sharp gasp. "You knew?"

He shook his head. "A good guess, now confirmed."

"I'm sorry, Garret. We both felt horrible that it happened. We didn't want to hurt you."

He accepted that with a nod. "Don't hurt each other trying to figure things out. And don't wait like we did, Joss. Three years is way too long to keep your true feelings to yourself. If you care for him, tell him."

Amazingly, Joss smiled. "Maybe. We'll see. Go to Darcy and tell her…tell her good luck. Give her my best. Maybe we could be friends later. When the weirdness goes away."

Garret grinned, winked at her, then raced for the door. "Gram!"

DARCY COULDN'T BELIEVE her eyes when Rosetta and Marilyn Tulane entered her delivery room. Hot on their heels was a nurse.

"Ladies, I'm sorry, but you're going to have to wait in the waiting room."

Rosetta zeroed in on Darcy's bed and headed toward her without pause, leaving Marilyn to speak with the nurse. She took Darcy's hand and bent over the rail, giving her a motherly kiss and a glare. "Don't you ever think a party is more important than you."

"I didn't want to ruin your fun," she whispered, touched by the woman's words.

"Well, now the party is over and we're here."

She glanced at Garret's mother. "Um…"

Marilyn Tulane smiled at her. "Do you mind? Between Rosetta and me, we've both been through this many times. We'd like to help you if we can."

But Garret's *mother?*

"Darcy, what do you say?" one of the nurses asked. "Do they stay or go?"

Marilyn came to join Rosetta by the bed. Her expression softened when she got a good look at Darcy's tear-streaked face. "Or would you like someone else? Garret wants to come in—"

"No. Absolutely not."

"He said you didn't want to see him anymore." Rosetta looked as if she couldn't quite believe the news.

"I don't. I don't want to see him because it's not right. For either of us. He's—"

"Ladies, let's not upset her, please," Dr. Clyde

said, coming into the room. "Darcy has quite a bit on her plate as it is."

Marilyn nodded, her expression sad. "I understand. And all that can wait until later, but Garret can't stand the thought of you being here alone. If you send us out, he'll likely break the door down and make a scene. We'd love to keep you company and lend you our support, Darcy. Please?"

Darcy gripped Rosetta's hand, afraid to believe in the kindness she saw in their eyes. Afraid to think too much about why she'd been born to a mother who didn't want her around instead of someone like Rosetta or Marilyn who took on responsibilities not their own.

Ask and ye shall receive.

"Oh, Nana."

"Pardon, dear?"

"You can stay. I'd love for you to—" Tears filled her eyes, a lump the size of Texas in her throat. "Thank you." *Thank you.*

"Oh, honey."

Both women patted and fussed and assured her that no thanks were needed, and Darcy cried even harder because it was just too sweet. Too much. Their presence, their caring, their love for a stranger who'd crashed into their lives and caused so many problems.

Marilyn brushed her bangs out of her eyes. "We'll

get you through this, and when you hold your baby, it'll all be okay, Darcy. You'll see."

She doubted that. Nothing would ever be okay again after knowing these people, but she didn't argue. Couldn't when a pain started low in her back and spread, deep and hard, leaving her curled up on her left side on the bed. She closed her eyes and tried to breathe, felt someone surround her hand in a reassuring, comforting grip. Seconds later her other hand was taken—and she held tight to the mothers she'd always wanted.

TOBY HEARD HIM first. Head low, Garret sat on the floor of the L&D waiting room, staring at the secured doors and muttering to himself between curses. Unlike the night Toby had brought Maria in, the room was empty.

He hesitated briefly, then continued walking and lowered himself onto the floor beside Garret with a sigh.

"Haven't seen you in a while. Now twice in one night. You been lying low?"

"Just busy." He made the statement before he noticed Garret's expression, the knowledge in his friend's eyes. He suppressed a groan and braced himself for a blow, determined he wouldn't block it.

"You'd better treat her right, Tobe."

He decided it was a good thing he was sitting down. "What?"

"You heard me. You'd better treat Joss right. She's a good woman and if you don't get your butt in gear and—" Garret pulled a box from his pocket "—give her the ring you picked out for her, some other jerk will come along and claim her." He tossed the box up in the air.

Toby caught it instinctively.

"Harry hates you, you need to know that up-front. All hell is going to break loose when he finds out about you and Joss, but I think with the gallery and all this, she's finally ready to be her own woman and stand up to him. Take advantage of it."

Toby sat there. *Stunned* didn't begin to describe how he felt right now. "You, uh… What about you? You know…us?"

Garret rolled his head along the wall and shot him a glare. "I don't like it that you didn't speak up, but who am I to talk after falling for Darcy under the circumstances?"

Toby stared at the box in his hand. Opened it up and there it was. The ring he'd chosen for the woman he loved.

"You can pay me in installments, but everything about the partnership has to be fifty-fifty."

Flipping the lid closed again, he tucked it into the inside of his coat pocket. "Deal."

And then they waited.

CHAPTER TWENTY-FOUR

SIX HOURS LATER nurses swarmed into the room to break down the bed, and Dr. Clyde told Darcy to push. She thought it would be over then. Who knew it took so long to have a baby? After another forty-five minutes, she bore down one more time and the baby made its way into the world.

Dr. Clyde looked up, her eyes crinkling behind her glasses and mask. "Congratulations, Darcy. You have a beautiful baby girl."

Rosetta and Marilyn smiled and laughed and wiped away tears as they oohed and ahhed over the squirming bundle in the doctor's hands. Darcy watched them all, unable to believe the baby was finally here and feeling out of sorts and dizzy now that it was over.

"Would you want one of these ladies to cut the cord?"

The question stumped her. She glanced up at Rosetta. "If Nana was here, she'd be the one I'd ask, but— Would you want to? You don't have to. I understand if—"

"I would love to, Darcy."

The nurse draped a blanket over Darcy's knees to give her some modesty and then the older woman moved into position.

Marilyn dabbed at her eyes and alternately patted Darcy or else gushed over the baby still in the doctor's care. Her daughter continued to cry as she was briskly wiped of fluid and wrapped in warmed blankets, then Dr. Clyde gave Darcy her daughter. "Support her head, yes, like that."

She was so light. So tiny. Her baby girl had blond hair like hers, long enough to curl at the ends, and her eyes were a dark, dark blue.

Tears trickled down Darcy's cheeks, but she smiled and laughed all the same. Ten tiny fingers and a button nose. Rosebud mouth. Definitely worth the pain.

Marilyn pulled her camera from her purse and snapped a shot of them gazing into each other's eyes. Another of Rosetta sitting beside her on the bed. One of each of them holding the baby, lots of her and her daughter together.

One of the nurses took the baby for its bath at the far end of the room, and Rosetta and Marilyn followed to watch, camera in hand, while Darcy stayed in the bed and tried to recover her composure while the linens were changed. She was a mom.

Dr. Clyde entered the room looking frazzled.

"Darcy, Mr. Tulane is outside and quite insistent. He'd like to come in."

Ignoring the questioning, concerned stares of the women across the room, she shook her head firmly back and forth. Sad and tired and happy all at once. "Would you tell him we're fine and that— Tell him Spike is a girl."

"Darcy, are you sure?" Rosetta asked. "He's been out there for hours, dear. Waiting to talk to you."

Darcy shook her head, not about to be dissuaded. Her daughter's birth was a new start. A new life. *I won't be her.* "I'm sure."

DARCY FROWNED at Rosetta. Using winter colds and the baby's near-term birth and risk of respiratory problems as an excuse, Darcy had managed to avoid visitors after being released from the hospital. Most especially Garret, much to his grandmother's upset. "I don't want to see him."

"He's been by every day since you came home."

Yes, he had. With gifts, no less. A pumpkin seat to put the baby in, a car-seat-stroller combo, a bassinet. Then there was the gigantic pink giraffe, enough baby toys for four families, including a rocking horse with a curly mane. There were gifts for her, too. A set of silk pajamas in brown—to match her eyes, the note read. A new CD she'd mentioned in passing. Flowers, lots of flowers.

Sunflowers and daisies—in *March*. And the last and boldest gift of all—business cards with her name on them, listing Nick's gym as her place of employment.

Once upon a time her entire life had fit in the storage compartments of her VW Beetle, allowing her to pick up and leave when and how she needed. Did stuff equal roots? "I haven't changed my mind."

The older woman frowned and went back to what she was doing, piling a third box full of donations from the residents of The Village.

"Rosetta, can't you understand why I find Garret's sudden turnaround questionable?"

"Of course I do. But you haven't seen him, Darcy. You don't know how haggard he looks. He's not sleeping, not eating much if at all. A man doesn't behave that way over a woman he *doesn't* love. He and Joss are no longer together."

"That has nothing to do with me."

"Oh, Darcy. How long are you going to punish him for being a caring man?"

She snuggled the baby closer, unable to respond.

"Garret loved Jocelyn in his own way, but I knew they weren't right together. They were too comfortable, like friends, which is what they've turned out to be. When you came along and I saw the way he looked at you, I knew. The way he loves you—"

"He doesn't love me."

"No? I disagree. How many men would've given up on you already? Do you know how many people go through their lives searching for that kind of love and never find it?" She left the toy-filled boxes and garbage bags by the door and moved to sit on the couch beside her. "Think of your mother. She's searching for it man by man and here you are throwing the real thing away. I think you're afraid to love him."

"Rosetta, please."

"I think," Garret's grandmother continued determinedly, "that after watching your mother make so many mistakes and having made one yourself with the baby's father, you're afraid to love. You think it won't last."

"It usually doesn't."

"Is that why you haven't named the baby yet?"

"Deciding on a name isn't easy."

"It isn't. But Garret mentioned your penchant for trying out names, and after all this time, I can't help but wonder if you're afraid to name the baby because it'll eliminate the distance you're keeping between you and your daughter."

"That's a horrible thing to say!"

"Am I wrong? You claim to want roots and a family, but when the perfect opportunity comes along in Garret and the baby, you back away. If you name your daughter, you'll feel a mother's emotions, a mother's love, and you're afraid it'll make you face all the things you still haven't faced about your mother."

"I know exactly who my mother is."

"Yes, you do know. But have you accepted it?"

How could anyone fully accept their mother's not wanting them? Wouldn't everyone want that attitude to change? Want a miracle to happen? *Reality bites, Darcy. When are you ever going to break those stupid rose-colored glasses?*

"You've been taught what *not* to do, Darcy. Motherhood makes you vulnerable in ways you've never imagined, but it also makes you strong. It binds your hearts and there's nothing like it, but you have to be open and want to experience it, to feel it. Are you going to let your mother rob you of loving your daughter? Rob you of a man worthy of your love and who loves you?"

Little by little Rosetta's words sank in. Was she letting that happen? She didn't intend to, but was she? She could lie to Rosetta until she was blue in the face, but she couldn't lie to herself. She was letting her fear of messing up overshadow her love, her feelings. Naming the baby…and loving Garret.

"What if I screw it all up?"

Rosetta smiled. "You'll make mistakes. You'll *all* make mistakes. If you let yourself love and forgive, it'll work out exactly as it's supposed to."

She stared down at her baby's sweet little face, the knot in her stomach growing.

"If you stop running from your past and the fear your mother instilled in you, if you face it, Darcy, you'll see the love you feel for Garret and your daughter is returned. But to receive it, you must first believe in it yourself."

Darcy buried her nose into her daughter's blankets, breathed in her baby smell. "Nana used to say something similar to that."

Rosetta nodded. "Because it's true, dear."

"Why did Garret move out of the house?"

"Why do you think? He wanted a place for you and the baby to come home to when you're ready."

"His job?"

"He's been frustrated working for Harry and was more than ready to quit. And when taking such a fresh step in life, why not go all the way? I've heard the office space above the gallery is coming along nicely. He and Toby will make a wonderful team."

"How do I know it's real? Two weeks ago Garret couldn't decide if he wanted me or not—"

"He knew, Darcy. But he had other responsibilities that needed to be taken care of before he could commit to you. He didn't know how to end things with Joss. He isn't a mean person, he didn't want to hurt her. Oh, Darcy, *think*. You knew where his heart was leading him. It's quite obvious he isn't the type of man to be with you if he didn't care for you, but now that he's free, you won't give him the time of day. Do you really think that's a coincidence?"

She could blame her hormones, her fears of becoming a mother, for her behavior. But the truth was she *ached* from missing Garret, wanted him in her life. Loved him. The way he smiled, the silly songs he sang. What was she *doing?*

A knock sounded at the door. "Rosetta?"

"That's Toby's mother. She's come to pick up the donations for Jocelyn while the boys work on the office."

Rosetta's words weighed on her mind. While Rosetta answered the door, Darcy carried the baby back down the hall to her bedroom. She laid the baby in the bassinet, then moved toward her dresser where the doll sat propped against the mirror. She stared down into Miss Potts's face a long time, memories sliding over her. She'd treasured Miss Potts for so long, but why? Why keep her when she represented everything that was bad in her life? A bad childhood, lack of emotional commitment from her mother.

Ready for a fresh start like Rosetta said, Darcy hurried down the hall to the only box left by the door and put the doll inside. Out with the past, in with the future. She wouldn't let her fear override the gifts she'd been given. The life she had to lead if only she were brave enough.

Back in the bedroom she sat on the edge of the bed and stared into her daughter's beautiful face. "Gram's right," she whispered, using the name Rosetta insisted the baby would use. "It's time to stop running. Time to start believing and being the person I want to be. The mommy you need me to be, not my mother's daughter. I won't get it right all the time, but…I'll do my best." She smoothed her fingertips over her daughter's downy head. "So, before I go and tell Garret how much I love him and want him, what do you think about Elizabeth? You could go by Elizabeth or Beth, Eliza or Lizzie. Liz. You'd have a lot of options and," she added, "it's Gram's middle name and she's the best great-grandma you could ever possibly have. Do you like it?"

"I love it."

Darcy gasped and turned to see Garret in the doorway, looking just as haggard as Rosetta said he did, the doll in his hand. She got to her feet, her trembling legs barely able to hold her. He wore jeans and a pullover, both loose and hanging on him.

He lifted the doll. "Why are you getting rid of this?"

"Because she's part of the past and I want to concentrate on the future…with you," she whispered. "If you still want me."

Raw hope crossed his face. "Sweetheart, I've

always wanted you. That hasn't been the problem. You love me?"

She nodded shakily.

"No, you've got to say it. I need to hear it. Do you love me?"

"Yes."

Some of the tension in his face eased. "Dream about waking up beside me for the next fifty years?"

"Yes."

He took a step closer, his eyes fierce. "Making love to you?"

"*Yes.*"

"Do you believe I want you—only you—because I love you and…Spike?"

He said that with a grin, a heart-stopping, love-filled smile that stole the breath right out of her lungs. Garret had given up every constant in his life—his girlfriend, his job—for her. All for her and her baby girl. He'd put them first. He'd put them *first.* It was romantic in the movies, but it was more romantic when it really happened. More special. More…amazing.

"Darcy?" Garret opened his arms and she flew across the room, slammed into him but knew he'd catch her, hold her. Love her. Because she finally understood what she hadn't been able to before meeting Garret.

"I love you, Darcy." He buried his nose in her

neck and inhaled. "Ahh, I've missed the way you smell. The way you feel. Not being able to see you has been killing me."

She swallowed, unable to believe she'd come so close to losing everything she'd ever wanted. "I know. I've missed you, too," she whispered, drawing back to trail her fingertips over his mouth. "I see it now."

"See what?"

Smiling through her tears, she leaned forward and kissed him, slow and deep, not breaking contact until they both breathed heavily. "I see that Nana's always right."

EPILOGUE

DARCY HAD NEVER GIVEN much thought to being a June bride, but she and Garret were married the second Saturday in June, five months to the day from when Garret rescued her. Rosetta was her matron of honor, Toby Garret's best man. She and Elizabeth wore white—just to give the gossips more to talk about—at her husband's insistence.

"Penny for your thoughts," Garret murmured later that evening, his arms sliding around her waist and turning her so that she snuggled against him. "Darcy, you okay, sweetheart?"

"I'm better than okay. I'm happy. Blessed. It's amazing." And even though her mother hadn't come to the ceremony, she was *still* okay, happy and blessed. Her love for Garret and Lizzie, for Garret's family, made it okay. Because she felt like her family *had* all been there. Garret's brothers and sister had flown in for the ceremony, his many aunts and uncles, cousins. So many cousins! It would take years to learn all their names.

Garret's fingers speared into her loose hair and he lifted her head so his mouth could close over hers.

"Mmm." He tasted of champagne and buttercream icing, desire and hard, hot man. His tongue coaxed her, eased her into a deeper, more possessive caress.

She fingered the buttons on his tuxedo shirt and then began unbuttoning them, hungry, needy, wanting her husband the way she'd never wanted anyone. His hands slipped out of her hair, pulled down the zipper in the back of her dress, but she didn't notice him tugging on the thin, spaghetti straps until the cool air made her shiver. She lowered her hands, one at a time, and let the white silk drop to the floor, aided by his hands. Garret shook. She could feel him trembling, and it touched a place deep, deep inside, burrowed into her heart, her soul. Love could hurt, took an extraordinary amount of trust, but when it was right, it was so, so right.

Garret dropped his head to her neck, scoring her skin with his teeth just hard enough to send goose bumps over her entire body, make her nipples pucker. He chuckled huskily when he felt her response. "Still sensitive there, huh? Let's see where else."

It was a game they'd played a lot since declaring their feelings. Every time he bared more of her, his head lowered, his lips, teeth and tongue alternatively kissing, nipping or sucking at her until it was all she could do to remain on her feet. His hands roamed over her full breasts and around to the clasp of her strapless bra. Down to push her panties away until the only things she wore were her spiky, sparkly heels and lace-topped, thigh-high stockings.

"I think we'll leave those on." Her husband's green eyes were heated, filled with love and desire, all for her. Pulling at his shirt, he held her gaze as he removed it. "I know what to expect, Darcy." A small smile formed on his mouth. He nodded toward the bed and she followed his stare, searching until she spotted the bottle of gel Garret had purchased to ensure her comfort. They'd waited to make love, pleasuring each other in different ways while they grew even closer and made things official, giving her body plenty of time to heal from giving birth.

Smiling ruefully, she reached for his belt and unfastened the catch, the snap of his pants. Garret took care of the zipper, and she slid her palms around his waist beneath the band, smiling when she heard him release a husky groan the moment her body touched his full length. She kissed his chest, sidled closer still, and relished the hiss he released when his arousal pressed against her stomach.

"You make me crazy." Garret's palms slid over her back, cupped her rump and squeezed. He kissed her, hard and fast and with dizzying thoroughness.

By the time Garret raised his head, she stood dazed, knees weak and wobbly, while he shucked his pants and underwear and gently pushed her backward until she sat on the edge of the king-size bed.

Kneeling on the floor in front of her with an appreciative leer, Garret arranged her just so, her legs on either side of him. Holding her gaze, his hands roamed. Her shoulders, the valley between her breasts. Her thighs. Back up again. Changing course, his fingers plucked at her nipples and rolled, drawing a sharp gasp from her because of the corresponding spear of desire that shot from her chest to her womb.

Garret leaned forward and fastened his lips over hers, leaving her awash with need. His stomach pressed against her warmth, and he slid an arm around her hips to pull her into closer contact, rubbing, teasing. Darcy squeezed her knees tight against his ribs to hold on to the sensation.

He trailed his lips lower, across the curve of her belly, lower, watching her with his passion-darkened gaze. Her heart pounded out of control, each breath harder to catch than the last because of the way he looked at her, unwavering as he pressed kiss after kiss lower over her stomach. Her belly button. Her thighs. She waited, never realizing how sensual it was to—

She gasped when he kissed her there, moaned because he stroked and laved, and pleasure overtook her until she couldn't think at all. Her hips lifted into the strokes, her lips parted to take in more air, and slowly, so slowly, her body began to tighten. Garret's excitement was tangible as he watched her responding to him, and she embraced the moment. Another stroke, two. Slow, decadent drags of his tongue in just the right spot that sent her skyward with a broken cry.

Time passed, she wasn't sure if it was seconds or minutes, but she slowly became aware of Garret's words of praise as he kissed his way back up her body.

"Beautiful. So beautiful."

She was vaguely aware of Garret moving onto the bed, using the bottle of lubricant generously to better ease his way. She caught her breath at the feel of him, the ridge of him inside her, a bit more, then tightness.

His breath rushed out of his chest. "Are you okay?"

She nodded, eyes closed due to the sensations bombarding her. He felt so good. So right. Like two halves of a whole. Tears stung, and she blinked rapidly.

"Darcy— Sweetheart."

"Don't stop."

"I don't want to hur—"

"You're not. I'm just…happy." She managed a watery smile. "I'm *happy,*" she repeated with a laugh. "I never thought I'd have this. You. *I love you.*"

She caught her breath when she saw the sheen of tears in his eyes before he closed them, felt the trembling inside him that revealed so much. He took her mouth in a powerful kiss, his hips moving in rocking motions, back and forth, until she slowly eased him all the way inside. They both groaned at the pressure, the sensation of him buried deep for the first time.

Garret kissed her, then set about pleasuring her all over again. She was amazed by the depth and breadth of this experience versus those of her past, relished the awareness because she knew she'd never treat Garret's love lightly having craved this for so long.

"Sweetheart, please. Ahh, you're killing me."

She smiled, lifted her knees around his hips and drove him deeper, tightened around him and pushed him over the edge. She savored his groans and the heat of his breath, the way he clutched her to him and held her like she was the most beautiful woman on earth—and she climaxed again.

Amazing.

She smiled up at the ceiling, her fingers in his hair, her mouth against his skin. *Amazing.* But then with Garret she'd come to expect nothing less. Garret and Elizabeth, her new family; they just proved that fairy tales could come true.

* * * * *

Look for the next
THE TULANES OF TENNESSEE
story by Kay Stockham!
Coming in July 2008 from
Harlequin Superromance

Enjoy a sneak preview of
MATCHMAKING WITH A MISSION
by B.J. Daniels,
part of the WHITEHORSE, MONTANA
miniseries.
Available from Harlequin Intrigue
in April 2008.

Nate Dempsey has returned to Whitehorse to uncover the truth about his past…

Nate sensed someone watching the house and looked out in surprise to see a woman astride a paint horse just on the other side of the fence. He quickly stepped back from the filthy second-floor window, although he doubted she could have seen him. Only a little of the June sun pierced the dirty glass to glow on the dust-coated floor at his feet as he waited a few heartbeats before he looked out again.

The place was so isolated he hadn't expected to see another soul. Like the front yard, the dirt road was waist-high with weeds. When he'd broken the lock on the back door, he'd had to kick aside a pile of rotten leaves that had blown in from last fall.

As he sneaked a look, he saw that she was still there, staring at the house in a way that unnerved him. He shielded his eyes from the glare of the sun off the dirty window and studied her, taking in her head of long blond hair that feathered out in the breeze from under her Western straw hat.

She wore a tan canvas jacket, jeans and boots. But it was the way she sat astride the brown-and-white horse that nudged the memory.

He felt a chill as he realized he'd seen her before. In that very spot. She'd been just a kid then. A kid on a pretty paint horse. Not this one—the markings were different. Anyway, it couldn't have been the same horse, considering the last time he had seen her was more than twenty years ago. That horse would be dead by now.

His mind argued it probably wasn't even the same girl. But he knew better. It was the way she sat the horse, so at home in a saddle and secure in her world on the other side of that fence.

To the boy he'd been, she and her horse had represented freedom, a freedom he'd known he would never have—even after he escaped this house.

Nate saw her shift in the saddle, and for a moment he feared she planned to dismount and come toward the house. With Ellis Harper in his grave, there would be little to keep her away.

To his relief, she reined her horse around and rode back the way she'd come.

As he watched her ride away, he thought about the way she'd stared at the house—today and years ago. While the smartest thing she could do was to stay clear of this house, he had a feeling she'd be back.

Finding out her name should prove easy, since he figured she must live close by. As for her interest in Harper House… He would just have to make sure it didn't become a problem.

* * * * *

Be sure to look for
MATCHMAKING WITH A MISSION
and other suspenseful Harlequin Intrigue stories,
available in April
wherever books are sold.

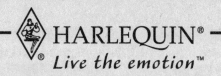

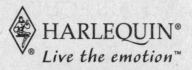

HARLEQUIN®
INTRIGUE®

BREATHTAKING ROMANTIC SUSPENSE

Shared dangers and passions lead to electrifying
romance and heart-stopping suspense!

Every month, you'll meet six new heroes
who are guaranteed to make your spine tingle
and your pulse pound. With them you'll enter
into the exciting world of Harlequin Intrigue—
where your life is on the line
and so is your heart!

THAT'S INTRIGUE—
ROMANTIC SUSPENSE
AT ITS BEST!

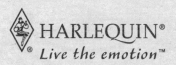

HARLEQUIN®
Live the emotion™

Harlequin® Historical
Historical Romantic Adventure!

*Imagine a time of chivalrous
knights and unconventional ladies,
roguish rakes and impetuous
heiresses, rugged cowboys
and spirited frontierswomen—
these rich and vivid tales will
capture your imagination!*

*Harlequin Historical . . .
they're too good to miss!*

HHDIR06